Home Before Dark

Heartlines

Heartlines

Margaret West

Home Before Dark

A Pan Original

First published 1988 by Pan Books Ltd,
Cavaye Place, London SW10 9PG
9 8 7 6 5 4 3 2 1
© Margaret West 1988
ISBN 0 330 30358 9
Printed and bound in Great Britain by
Richard Clay Ltd, Bungay, Suffolk

Chapter 1

I'd been sitting on a rock in the little deserted cove for ages, staring out to sea, wishing myself miles away from here. The vessel that had been a vague shape in the fading light was coming in towards the shore, and I blinked as I saw it more clearly. It was a sailing ship with two masts, and looked like an old pirate ship.

It slowed as it neared the rocky outcrop that formed one side of the horseshoe bay, and disappeared, as if it had been swallowed up by the reef. Somewhere along the coast, I thought, there must be some sort of regatta, with people sailing replicas of old sailing ships. And there must be a channel through which it had gone to the adjoining bay. I thought about walking along to see how it had managed to slip out of sight, but the tide was turning. I'd look some other time.

I scrambled down off the rock and began to walk back towards the cliff path, when I noticed something black and shiny, half hidden by a rock among the pools. Probably a dead sea bird, but it might just be a seal. Seals were sometimes seen on this coast.

As I climbed and slithered over the rocks, I saw that the black shape looked more like fur than feathers – so it could be a seal!

I leapt on to a patch of firm sand, and caught my breath in a sob. It was a large black dog with a gentle face — and it was dead!

I touched the limp ears where the hair was glistening wet, as scalding tears raced down my cheeks. Typical of this place, I thought! You hope to see something beautiful, like a baby seal, and you find a lovely big black dog which has fallen down the cliff to its death!

I stroked the lifeless head, wondering what to do. Someone would be looking for him, going frantic with worry.

Then, above the pounding of the waves and the whining of the wind, I heard a faint sound, and blinked the tears from my eyes. Brown eyes were looking up at me, full of hope, and a warm tongue was trying to lick my hand.

'You're alive!' I gasped, and felt for his collar to see if there was an address on it, but the dog whimpered with pain, so I laid my hand on his head gently, and talked to him quietly. He was too big for me to carry up the cliff path. I'd have to leave him and run to the vet's house.

I pulled off my anorak and wrapped it around the dog, trying to explain that I'd have to leave him, but that I'd come back as quickly as I could. The brown eyes implored me, but, as he tried to move, to follow me, the dog fell back with a yelp of pain.

'Don't move,' I said gently. 'Stay! I promise I'll come back.'

Feeling like a traitor, I turned and ran, scrambling back up the cliff path, cutting my knee on a rock, eventually stumbling on to the road, where I took a breath and began to run.

I heard a voice calling to me, but I couldn't stop. A tall figure in a red sweater leapt from a tractor and raced after me, calling 'What's wrong? *Wait*! What's happened?'

'There's a dog,' I choked, as he reached me. 'Badly hurt, on the beach. I have to get the vet.'

'Whereabouts? Stop, please — just one moment. I'll go down to the dog. You go for the vet.'

I stopped and pointed over the cliff edge to the rock that hid the dog from our view. 'Look for a blue anorak,' I panted.

My chest hurt as I reached the open gate of the vet's house. His Land Rover was just coming down the drive. 'Lorna? You want me?' he called, drawing up beside me.

'Quick, Mr Evans,' I gasped. 'Dog on the beach, badly hurt.'

'Get in,' he said briskly, then, as I slid into the passenger seat, 'Grab that jacket that's on the back seat and put it on. You shouldn't be out without a coat in this wind.'

The Land Rover bumped over the rough ground to the cliff edge, and soon we were beside the dog, who looked up at me and thumped his tail, once.

The boy from the tractor was kneeling beside the dog. He looked up and said, 'Hi, Dad! It's Peter's labrador — Jack.' The vet gave the dog an injection and the brown eyes closed.

An hour later, we were in the warm kitchen of the vet's house, drinking scalding coffee. The dog was still unconscious in the surgery, with one leg in plaster and bandages holding dressings on to various parts of his body. David Evans, the vet, said he'd make a full recovery, but it would take time.

'If you hadn't found him,' he said, 'he'd have died of exposure, or been washed out to sea when the tide came in.'

I was wearing a sweater belonging to the boy from the tractor who'd turned out to be the vet's son, Gwillym, whom I'd never met before. I hadn't realized, until we'd finished attending to the dog, that my sweater was covered in blood. I'd been wondering why the sight of a girl running should have signalled danger to Gwillym. Now I realized what I must have looked like!

'Well, and how are you settling in here?' the vet asked. 'A month you've been here now, isn't it?'

Avoiding the question, I said, 'How did you know my name? I knew yours because I pass this house often, and your name's on the brass plate by the gate, but we've never met before.'

He smiled, and I noticed how alike father and son were. Gwillym was about eighteen, and had the same very dark hair and dark brown eyes as Mr Evans. They had the same smile which showed perfect white teeth against a tanned skin.

'Someone in the village pointed you out to me,' Mr Evans answered. 'We're curious about newcomers. I met your parents at a parish council meeting in the church hall.'

I nodded. 'They went there to get to know people.'

'And what about you? Have you made many new friends?'

I was saved from answering by a frenzied banging on the back door. Gwillym got up, murmuring, 'Not another emergency?'

It was the dog's owner, who'd been out searching for him and had just found out what had happened. I could hear his voice, hoarse with anxiety, and Gwillym's voice, calm, reassuring, with the attractive Welsh lilt in it. I liked the way the local people spoke, with music in their voices, and the words pronounced so clearly.

'Peter Jackson is a sculptor,' Mr Evans told me. 'He lives alone in that cottage half a mile down the coast road from here. He and Jack are inseparable.'

A sculptor. So I imagined a scruffy, middle-aged man, with an untidy beard and straggly hair. The man who came into the kitchen, his face white and anxious, was about twenty-five, I thought, clean shaven, with fair hair casually styled.

He took my hand in both of his. 'Gwillym told me what you did,' he said. 'How can I ever thank you? What can I do – apart from buying you a new anorak, of course, and a new sweater too, if that's yours in a polythene bag in the lobby?'

'No!' I protested. 'I'll get the anorak cleaned. I have another one to wear. The sweater will wash clean if I soak it first in cold water – and it's only an old thing anyway.'

Gwillym was handing Peter a mug of coffee, so he let go of my hand, but he went on looking at me, as if he wanted to remember my face for ever. I felt my cheeks growing warm with embarrassment, and Gwillym

9

said, 'Sit down, Peter. All's well that ends well.'

'What was Jack doing, out on his own, anyway?' Mr Evans asked.

Peter sighed. 'Courting, I expect. It's that golden retriever at Jones's farm. Every so often, Jack is overcome with love for her, and before I know it, he's gone to find her.'

I glanced at my watch. 'It's time I went,' I said. 'I'll just get my anorak—'

'No,' Peter said. 'I've got it. I'll return it to you when it's been cleaned. I'll drive you home, and please wear my jacket, though it'll be a bit large.' He was unzipping his leather jacket as I protested that Gwillym had already lent me an anorak, and that my house was only three minutes' walk away.

'I know your house,' Peter nodded, following me into the hall, where Gwillym held his anorak for me, and I slipped my arms into the sleeves which covered my hands completely. 'You live at Applegarth – that lovely old stone house.'

I stared at him. 'How do you know that?'

Mr Evans laughed. 'Everyone here knows! Applegarth has been empty for so long that we were all glad to see a nice family move in and bring it to life again.'

Bring it to life, I thought; that rambling, cold, draughty old place, where all the doors squeaked as you opened them? But I smiled and nodded. I'd never understand these people.

In Peter's car, I huddled into Gwillym's anorak and asked, 'What sort of sculpture do you do? We went on a school trip to see the Henry Moore exhibition last year. Is your work like that?'

He smiled. 'I have to earn a living,' he answered. 'I do whatever people are willing to pay for. I like doing portraits of people – head and shoulders.'

I frowned in surprise. 'I thought sculptors did what they wanted to do, and had exhibitions, and people came and bought their work.'

He laughed aloud. 'Oh, Lorna! How wonderful that would be! Most of us work very hard for other people before we can spare any time for our own work. I'm employed by architects who want a piece of sculpture for a new building, and if I'm lucky I get commissioned to do a portrait of someone. Come and see my studio sometime. You know where it is?'

I nodded. 'Thank you. I'd love to come.'

'Bring your parents, if they're interested,' he said. 'I met your father in the pub the other evening and he mentioned that he'd like to see my work.'

There it was again! This complete stranger knew my father!

'I'll never be out of your debt, Lorna,' Peter murmured. 'Did Dai Evans tell you that Jack was *thrown* over the cliff?'

I sat up, stiff with horror. 'No! I thought he'd fallen over! How did Mr Evans know? Who would do a dreadful thing like that?'

'Dai could tell by the injuries,' Peter replied. 'I could murder Dylan for this!'

'Dylan?' I repeated, chilled by the tone of his voice.

'It must have been Dylan,' he said. 'Jones's farm goes up to the cliff edge in places. Dylan has a filthy temper.'

11

I shuddered. What sort of man threw a dog over a cliff? 'Will you tell the police?' I asked.

He shook his head. 'It would only cause trouble for Griffith Jones – he's the farmer, you know. And I'm in the wrong. I should have made sure Jack didn't get out, but he would never harm sheep, or anything like that. He just gets desperate to see Griffith Jones's retriever now and again.'

I knew how Jack felt. I was desperate to see Mike, and he was miles away, in London. Only a month ago, I'd been there too, seeing him every day, never dreaming that we'd be parted like this.

As I went into the house, Mum came into the hall, looking anxious. 'Where've you been?' she demanded. 'That isn't your anorak you're taking off! Where did you get that sweater? It's much too large – or is it a new fashion to wear them down to your knees?'

I told her briefly what had happened, and, as I went upstairs to get another sweater, she called after me, 'Oh, Lorna! Mrs Llewellyn brought this letter. It was delivered to their house by mistake and they've been away for a fortnight. By the postmark, it's been lying on their doormat for two weeks!'

I dashed back downstairs and almost snatched the letter from her. 'Only one?' I asked. 'You're sure there's only one?'

'Yes. One for you and one for Dad. That's all.'

The letter had a Wimbledon postmark, and the writing was Mike's. My heart was pounding as I ran up to my bedroom and flung myself on the bed, my hands trembling as I ripped open the envelope.

It wasn't a long letter — just one page of Mike's big black scrawl.

'Dear Lorna,

Thanks for your letters. Sorry I didn't get around to replying earlier. What a crummy place Caeraddon sounds to be!

'Everything here is much the same. I saw Helen and Rob the other day. Helen said you were coming up for the weekend to her sister's eighteenth birthday party, so I'll see you then. Helen said she'd phoned you about arrangements and you sounded really fed up with that place.

'Now you're sixteen, no-one can make you live at home any more, so why don't you just leave? You could get a job here, in London, and we could find you a bed-sitter or something.

'Looking forward to seeing you again soon,

'With much love, Mike.'

I pressed the letter to my cheek and closed my eyes, trying to picture his face. Thick fair hair, grey eyes, straight nose, firm mouth, and a smile that made my heart turn over.

I'd known Mike for ages, at school, but only really noticed him when he played the part of Hamlet in the school end of term production. At that time he'd been going around with Zara Harrison, who can have any boy she fancies — you know the type! Mike's tall and fantastic-looking, and I thought Zara would hang on to him for ever, but they broke up. I managed to get into conversation with him at our local Friday disco, and he stayed with me all evening, then took me home.

After that, we were always together. People started linking our names, asking us to parties together. Mike and Lorna. It was wonderful.

I thought I'd die when the rumours about Dad's firm relocating came true. Of all the awful words in the English language, "relocation" must be the worst! It ought to apply to nuts and bolts and things – not people.

My whole family had been relocated, along with the firm, to this tiny Welsh village. In fact the firm was near Gwenally, the nearest town, but most of the people had chosen to live in the surrounding countryside.

My two young brothers were overjoyed. 'Magic!' 'Brill!' was how they described everything, from the wild orchard behind the old house, to the rock-strewn beach at the foot of the cliff. They were actually looking forward to starting at new schools at the end of this summer holiday!

Soon, I'd have to take the bus to the old Grammar school in Gwenally, and when I thought about it, my stomach twisted into a tight knot.

For the first few days, Mum and Dad had worn uneasy, hopeful smiles, as they'd unpacked boxes and talked about redecorating the house, but now they were into local events, passing on gossip, as if the people here were really interesting.

Most of my things were still in big cardboard boxes we'd got from the supermarket in Wimbledon. I'd hung my clothes in the wardrobe and taken out Mike's photo which was on my bedside table in the silver frame Gran had given me, which she'd had for ages. Beside it was the china cat he'd bought for me from a stall in Covent Garden one Saturday, the coral necklace he'd brought back for me from Spain, and another framed photograph of both of us standing by his car.

I got up and put on the record he'd bought me when we'd first started going out together. I played it all the time. I needed to. 'Flip Side of Loving' had never made the charts, but it was the tune we first danced to at the disco, and it brought him nearer to me. Mike had it on cassette and I wondered if he often played it, too, and thought of me.

Mum was calling up that dinner would soon be ready, and I read Mike's letter again before changing into one of my own sweaters and folding Gwillym's. I'd wash it and return it when I took back his anorak.

A part of Mike's letter kept coming back to my mind, as if the words were burned there, so that, if I closed my eyes, I could see the big black handwriting. 'Why don't you just leave? You could get a job in London, and we could find you a bed-sitter or something.'

A thrill of excitement ran right through me. A bed-sitter of my own, where I could do exactly as I liked, and never have to tell anyone where I was going, or what time I'd be home! I pictured it, small and cosy, with Mike sitting in an armchair, relaxing, while I cooked a meal for us both.

Then I sighed. I had to stay at school and take 'A' levels, so that I could go to university, or college. The idea of leaving school and getting a job had never once occurred to me. But — why not? Because Mum and Dad wouldn't hear of it, that was why not. I shuddered at the thought of telling them I wanted to leave home. Surely they could stop me?

I picked up the letter again and read, 'Now you're sixteen, no one can make you live at home any more . . . ' Could that be true? There must be some way I could find out for certain.

The cold, bleak hopelessness that I'd lived with since we came here to this house, lifted as I folded the letter and put it under my pillow. Today was Wednesday. On Friday, I'd be in London, staying at Helen's house, and I'd see Mike again — actually *be* with him! Maybe I wouldn't come back here at all!

Dad was home, and as we all sat down to our evening meal, Mum made me repeat the story of how I'd found the dog.

My two brothers, Andrew and William, listened with interest, for a change. Andrew is ten and wants to join the Navy. William is twelve and wants to be an artist.

'Gwillym Evans is going to art school after the holidays,' I told him. 'I think he said Cardiff. Wherever it is, he can live at home and travel there every day.'

Mum nodded. 'That's good. His father would be lonely if Gwillym went away. Gwillym's mother died when he was quite young.'

I gazed at her, amazed. How on earth did she know that? Maybe she even knew who Dylan was. I intended to avoid him at all costs, and to warn the boys to keep away from him.

'Peter's dog,' I said, 'was actually *thrown* over the cliff, by someone called Dylan, who, I think, works for Mr Jones at the farm.'

The boys' eyes grew wide as they stared at me, and Mum gasped, 'What a dreadful thing to do! I hope the police will deal with him! Perhaps he's not quite sane though – to do a wicked thing like that.'

It was a moment before I realized that Dad was grinning, and we all turned to stare at him as if he'd changed into a monster.

'Dylan,' he said, 'is the name of Mr Jones's prize bull. The vet would know by the wounds on the dog that a bull had tossed him.'

I sighed with relief. The anger I'd seen in Peter's eyes was for a bad-tempered bull, not a man, and there wasn't a dangerous lunatic running around Caeraddon.

Mum said, 'Gwillym is helping Mr Jones on the farm during the holidays.'

I nodded. 'He was driving a tractor when he saw me running for the vet.'

'If he's artistic, he'll be interested in Peter Jackson's sculpture,' Mum added.

'Yes. He sometimes helps Peter in his studio,' I replied, wondering what this had to do with anything.

'I'll wash his pullover tonight,' Mum said. 'Then you can return it, and his anorak, tomorrow. He should be in in the evening. Such a nice boy! You remember Gwillym, Steve?'

Dad blinked and said, 'Do I? Oh yes! The boy who was helping with the flower show the first week we arrived here. Very dark hair – very like his father.'

'Yes,' Mum agreed warmly. 'A very good-looking boy, and so friendly and helpful.'

And then it dawned on me! She was for ever telling me that I must join in local activities and get to know people. She said I could invite Mike down for a weekend, but not until the spare room was ready. If I became interested in Gwillym, that would solve everything!

It wouldn't. I'd met three nice people this afternoon, but this was still Caeraddon, quiet and gloomy, like a graveyard. Soon, I was going back to London, and Mike.

Chapter 2

Later that evening, when Mum and Dad were out for a couple of hours, and the boys were in bed, I phoned Helen. I just had to talk to someone about Mike's letter. I read out the bit where he suggested I could leave home.

'What d'you think?' I asked. 'I mean – couldn't Mum and Dad *make* me come home and go back to school?'

'I don't know!' she gasped. 'Oh, Lorna – would you really do it? Actually *leave home*?'

She was astonished, then excited, then she said how marvellous it would be if she could leave school too.

'We could share a flat,' she exclaimed. 'I think I could get a job as a waitress at that restaurant where I had that holiday job! Oh, but it's hopeless for me! I *know* my parents would go raving mad. I'd never be able to stand it. Tell you what, though – Susan's boyfriend, Roger, works in a solicitor's office. We could ask him to find out about the law – whether you'd be allowed to live away from home. We'll ask him at the party on Saturday night.'

After talking to Helen, I wrote a letter to Mike. I'd written to him lots of times, but all I'd got from him was this one short letter. Well – lots of people hate writing letters. Mum said I could only ring London in the evenings, after six o'clock, when it was cheaper, and each time I'd phoned Mike's house, he was out. Sometimes no one answered the phone at all, but when his mother answered she always said, 'He's not here, I'm afraid. I don't expect him back until after eleven.' Well, I couldn't ring after eleven, could I? Mum said people didn't like it if you phoned that late when they might have gone to bed. Dad always said that whatever needed to be discussed on the phone after half past ten in the evening could wait until morning. I couldn't risk annoying Mike's parents.

In my letter, I said I'd been thinking seriously about his suggestion, and explained that his letter had been misdirected, so I'd only got it today.

'It's given me new hope,' I wrote. 'Maybe, after all, we will be together again soon.'

I found a first class stamp and dashed across the road to the post box, almost opposite the house. He'd get the letter on Friday morning, and I'd be seeing him in the evening.

That night, I lay in bed, reliving the last few hours Mike and I had spent together, the night before we moved down here.

It was a lovely summer evening, and we'd walked hand in hand in Richmond Park. I could hardly speak for the misery which made my throat tight, and there was a dull ache in my chest.

'Ring me tomorrow,' he said, 'when you get there. Where is it? Caernarvon?'

'Caeraddon,' I'd mumbled.

But our phone hadn't been connected, so I'd trekked to the call box in the village. The line was crackly, and neither of us could think of anything to say. I said I'd ring again when our phone was working, and went home and wrote the first of my long letters to him.

A nagging worry that I kept pushing to the back of my mind resurfaced. How could Mike be out every single evening when I phoned – even when I phoned at exactly one minute past six? Where did he go – *without me*? I'd never met his parents, which was a bit strange, because Mike had been to our house lots of times. Mrs Kingston always sounded fed up when she answered the phone, as if she'd been expecting someone important, and it was only me. Otherwise, I could have asked her to ask him to ring me.

I closed my eyes and thought of the weekend I'd be spending at Helen's house. We'd catch up on all the gossip about people at school . . . I'd see Mike again . . .

Next morning, Mum and I were having coffee when there was a knock at the door and I answered it.

A man was standing there, holding a huge bouquet of yellow roses. 'Miss Lorna Collins?' he asked.

'Yes. But – there's some mistake,' I gasped, as he thrust the bouquet into my arms, smiled, ran back to his van, and drove off.

When I remembered to look for the card it said, 'For Lorna, with deepest gratitude, from Peter and Jack.'

As I arranged the roses in three vases, William called out to Andrew, 'Hey! You know that dog that Lorna rescued? He's sent her some flowers. Must have phoned the shop and used his credit card.'

They fell about with laughter, and Mum exclaimed over the roses, and reminded me about taking back Gwillym's sweater and anorak.

I didn't mind. The flowers were the first really nice thing that had happened to me since I arrived in Caeraddon. They made me feel different – sophisticated. Certainly not like a schoolgirl. Yellow roses! Long stems with no thorns!

I rolled up the yellow ribbon that had tied the bouquet, smoothing out the creases, and put it, with the card, into my dressing table drawer. I'd keep it for ever. Long after the flowers had died, I'd remember that someone had sent me yellow roses, and I'd feel cool and elegant, and graceful, and over twenty, at least.

After lunch, I'd go to Peter's cottage and thank him

for the flowers, and find out how Jack was progressing, in the vet's hospital, where he had to stay for a time.

I'd return Gwillym's anorak and sweater on the way there. If Peter was busy, I wouldn't interrupt him. I'd just say how beautiful the flowers were, and that I'd always loved yellow roses. Then I'd leave, gracefully — in a sophisticated manner.

Andrew was nagging me to go up to the attic and look through his telescope, which Dad had bought him in Gwenally, for his birthday, the day after we arrived here. He spent hours up there, looking out to sea.

'It's *great*!' William said. 'Better than Dad's field glasses.'

There were two large empty attics at the top of the house. In one of them, Andrew had set up his telescope on an old table in front of the gable window. He had a notebook, which he called his "logbook" in which he was recording everything he saw, practising, no doubt, for the Navy.

'Twiddle this bit here,' he said, ''till you get a clear view, and you can swing it right round.'

It was amazing! There was a fishing boat on the horizon, and I could see the men on deck! I could see beyond our cove into the next bay, where a group of children were collecting shells. All along the coast there were secluded inlets on either side of our bay. I swung the telescope to bring Peter's cottage into view. Like our house, it was set well back from the road, surrounded by trees — a small, red-roofed white house, with a garden at the back.

'Isn't it absolutely *ace*?' Andrew asked excitedly.

'It's the best present I've ever had, in my *whole*, *entire* life!'

William was beside me, with Dad's field glasses, pointing out the vet's house. 'Look – that extension at the back, painted white, is the animal hospital where animals have to stay after operations. The dog you saved will be in there.'

I adjusted the telescope to bring closer objects into sharp focus.

'Isn't that the guy with the funny name that Mum keeps going on and on about?' William asked.

'Oh yes!' It was as if Gwillym was only yards away from me as he walked from the Land Rover into the house. In blue jeans and green sweater, he really was, as Mum had pointed out, very good-looking – if you liked dark men.

'It's not a funny name,' I said. 'In fact, I think it's the same name as yours. I think Gwillym is Welsh for William – or the other way about.'

'Come to the other window,' Andrew was urging me. 'Let me move the telescope for you.'

He carried it very carefully, setting it on the wide window sill of the opposite window that looked out over the orchard at the back of the house. 'There,' he said proudly. 'Look now.'

I could see the straggle of little shops that wound up the hill towards the church. I could even read the names over the shops.

'See the school?' Andrew asked. 'Turn it – go on – further. That's my school, where I'm going. See it now?'

23

The school was Victorian, small and compact in grey stone, with a bell on top and an asphalt playground. 'It's a "rural" school,' Andrew explained. 'Only fifty nine pupils, so I'll know absolutely everyone, and I'll be in the top form, with the oldest boys and girls. Come and look at my logbook.'

In the logbook, I read such entries as, "18.00 hrs. Farmer Jones took cows in for milking. 12.00 hrs. Mrs Thomas hung out washing. 4 vests. 4 pairs breefs, 12 socks, 5 shirts. 20.00 hrs. Motor cruser went past. 19.30 hrs. Brig went into cliff side."

'What's a brig?' I asked. 'And that's not how you spell cruiser, or briefs.'

'A brig is a two-masted sailing ship,' Andrew answered. 'Square sails on the foremast, and fore-and-aft sails on the mainmast.'

I was impressed. He seemed to know a lot about ships.

William said, 'But – you can't have seen a ship like that, Andrew. They're old. Like in history.'

'I saw one like that yesterday,' I said, 'when I was on the beach, just before I saw the dog. Don't they use them for training ships sometimes?'

'I hope so,' Andrew said. 'I want to sail on a ship like that. With sails. When I join the Navy.'

William was looking at the logbook. 'Went into cliff side?' he read. 'What's that mean?'

'It disappeared,' Andrew answered.

'It did look like that,' I nodded. 'There must be a channel it went through into the next bay.'

I flicked the pages. Andrew had seen the sailing ship four days ago. I saw it yesterday.

'Maybe it's a ghost ship,' William said. 'There used to be pirates around this coast, and smugglers. Mr Jones told me. Maybe it's the ghost of a ship that was wrecked.'

'Well don't get ideas about diving for treasure,' I told him.

'Isn't it *great*, living here?' William murmured, focusing the field glasses again. 'Why don't you like it, Lorna? Everyone talks to you here. Mr Jones is going to look in his attic for a kite for Andrew, and Mrs Morgan at the newsagents' in the village gave him some out-of-date sailing magazines, and she gave me a big pile of old motoring magazines. Nobody ever took any notice of us at home – except people we knew, of course.'

'M'm,' I murmured, turning the telescope past the village towards a patch of woodland. 'What's that huge white house over there?' I asked.

'That's the Price's place,' William answered. 'They're *enormously* rich. They have a Rolls Royce and a Porsche, and they have guard dogs on their land.'

'Everything the Prices have cost a very high price,' Andrew giggled, as he carried the telescope back to the table. William and I groaned, and Andrew said, 'Anyone not laughing at my jokes is not allowed to look through my telescope.'

'That's the whole of Caeraddon, deprived of snooping then,' William muttered, still gazing through Dad's field glasses.

I could see how I could get addicted to this as I took one last look through the telescope, turning it to the left, looking along the coast.

Peter backed his car into his drive, got out, and took a heavy sack from the boot, which he carried into the house.

I stood up. 'That's it,' I said firmly. 'I could sit here for hours and turn into a village gossip. Thanks for letting me look, Andrew. It really is brill.'

'Come up and look any time,' he said generously. 'If I'm busy logging something, you can look through the field glasses till I'm free.'

After lunch, I set out for Peter's cottage, calling at the vet's house on the way, to hand in Gwillym's sweater and anorak. A cheerful-looking woman answered the door, and promised to thank Gwillym for me, for the loan of his things. She told me she came every day to cook, and look after the house for Mr Evans.

Peter's studio was a low building, built on to the back of his cottage, which I hadn't been able to see through the telescope because it was screened by tall trees.

I could see Peter through the open door and he turned and looked really pleased to see me as he welcomed me in. I stepped on to a stone floor in a room lit by windows all along the length. In the centre of the room, on a dais, was a group of figures, life-size. There was a man, a woman, and a toddler. The child was running, and the woman was reaching out, her fingers touching his shoulder, ready to grab his shirt, as I remembered Mum reaching out to catch Andrew when he was little. The man had his arm around the woman's waist, and his gaze was directed at the child.

'I call this, "Family Group",' Peter smiled. 'Not

brilliantly original, but that's what it is. It's for a large office block just outside London.'

'Oh!' I exclaimed. 'It ought to be in a park, where lots of people can see it. It's made of clay. I thought you'd work in stone.'

'I do work in stone, sometimes,' he answered. 'This will be cast in bronze when it's finished.'

There were smaller pieces of his work on shelves all around the room, mostly figures in various poses, and a few abstract shapes. Most of the models were in white plaster.

'These are copies,' Peter said. 'I keep them for reference. The originals have been done in bronze, or reconstituted marble. I'll show you photos of the original pieces.'

He made coffee while I looked at the photos in a large portfolio. 'Am I interrupting your work?' I asked anxiously. 'I don't want to be in the way, but I just had to come and thank you for the lovely flowers.'

'I want an excuse for a break,' he grinned. 'Sit down and tell me all about yourself.'

We went to the far end of the studio, where I sat in a comfortable old armchair, and Peter sat opposite me on a battered sofa. He set our coffee mugs on a table between us, and began looking at me intently, as he had done yesterday.

'I'm sorry,' he said suddenly. 'Was I staring at you? You have such an interesting face, Lorna. I'd like to do a portrait of you – head and shoulders. But I don't suppose you'd have time to sit for me, would you?'

'Oh!' I was staggered for a moment. 'You mean, like

those?' I pointed to a shelf where there were several busts, four of middle-aged men, one of a child, and another of a girl of about Peter's age, which wasn't finished. It was made of clay, and wrapped in polythene. I could see that the face was perfect, but that the hair wasn't smoothed like the rest of the work.

'Yes. Like those. The girl is Megan Price. Do you know her?'

'No. I've heard of people called Price who live in the large white house.'

'Yes. Megan and her father live all alone in that huge place – except for a housekeeper, cook, and people who come in each day to work on the gardens and so on. Megan gives fantastic parties. You'll like her when you meet her.'

'Oh – I don't expect I'll meet her.'

'I'll take you to her next party. A week on Saturday, I'll take you to the Price mansion and show you how the rich live!'

'Well, thanks, Peter, but – I might not be here then.'

'You're going away to school?'

'No. I'm supposed to be going to the girls' school in Gwenally in two weeks' time. But – well, I might go back and live in London.'

Why was I telling him this? It was still only a dream, anyway, and I'd told no one except Helen.

He nodded, waiting for me to go on, and suddenly, I was telling him everything – about having to leave all my friends, and the school where I was happy, and, most of all, about having to leave Mike. Then I added what had been in Mike's letter, and said I was thinking about leaving school and getting a job in London.

When I'd finished telling him, I caught my breath. 'You – you won't tell Mum and Dad, will you?' I asked.

He paused, frowning. 'Have you thought of discussing all this with them? If they know how unhappy you are, they might consider arranging for you to stay with someone they know, so you could go back to your old school.'

'No!' I gasped. 'No – they never would. Mum thinks I'm too young to have a steady boyfriend, and that I'll forget all about Mike, soon.'

'So it's just Mike, is it?' Peter asked. 'You hate Caeraddon because he isn't here.'

I shook my head. 'No. If Mike were here, he'd hate it too. There's nowhere to go, nothing to do. I mean – *you* don't actually *like* it here, do you?'

He smiled. 'Yes, I do. I'm a Londoner too. I've lived all my life in Highgate, and went to art school in London. I'd been here on holiday as a child, and when I couldn't find anywhere in London that I could afford, to live and work in, I came here.'

'It's different for you,' I murmured. 'Your work, and – well, it's different for older people, isn't it?'

He nodded. 'Yes. I can see what it's like for you.'

We didn't talk for a while. Peter was so easy to be with that you didn't feel uncomfortable if you weren't making conversation.

Then he said, 'What about a compromise, Lorna? Suppose you were to make a real effort to stick around here for, say, one term at school? You'd meet other girls and find out what goes on in Gwenally.'

I gazed at him dully. He didn't understand, after all. No one did.

'Dad took me into Gwenally,' I told him, 'to see the Headmistress of the girls' school. It's *awful*! The building is old and dark and gloomy, and I've never been with just girls before – though I don't mind that so much. My school at home is modern, all bright and light, and sort of – alive. The notice board, as you go in, is always full of leaflets and posters about what's going on – school outings, society meetings, lots of things happening.'

'You could try it out,' Peter said. 'It'll be just as different for your brother, at the boys' school.'

'But William is thrilled,' I exclaimed. 'All because they play rugger instead of football, and they've got a bigger art department. And Andrew is wild about the village school, and *they* haven't even got a proper science department. Dad was worried about that, until he talked to the headmistress. They keep chickens there, and rabbits, and a goat.'

'Sounds fun,' Peter smiled.

'If you're going to be a farmer,' I agreed. 'But Andrew wants to join the Navy.'

'Then he's in the right place here. When he's older he'll have a chance to do some sailing. What do you want to do for a career, Lorna?'

I sighed. 'I've no idea. Anyway, I've decided to leave school and just take any job I can get.'

Peter looked worried, and said, 'But Lorna – it's very hard for a girl on her own – especially in London.'

'I won't *be* on my own!' I gasped. 'I have lots of friends where I used to live.'

He reached out and took a drawing pad, and tore a corner off a sheet of paper, wrote something on it, and handed it to me. 'Here's my phone number,' he said quietly. 'If you do stay in London, and things go wrong – if you need help in any way at all – promise me that you'll ring me. I'll come straight away.'

I took the piece of paper and gazed at him, astonished. In London, I'd have Mike! – There'd be Helen, and all my other school friends, too. Why would I ever need to phone Peter for help?

'You – er – may not want to worry your parents,' he said, hesitantly. 'I mean – if you take a big step like this, there are bound to be snags. You may need an older person . . . Anyway, just remember, if things go wrong, I'm here, and I'll come.'

I pushed the paper into the pocket of my jeans. 'Thanks,' I smiled, 'but I really don't think—'

'You forget,' he grinned. 'I owe you.'

I laughed, suddenly understanding. 'You *don't*! That's crazy! All I did was what anyone would have done.'

'It was more,' he murmured seriously. 'You wrapped your anorak around Jack.'

'Well – he was so wet and cold, and I had to leave him to get help, and I felt awful because I couldn't explain that I'd be coming back, and—'

'It wasn't just the warmth of the coat that kept him going, Lorna,' Peter said. 'It was the scent of you, on the coat. Instinctively he trusted you, and you left your

31

scent with him, which reassured him, made him feel he wasn't alone.'

'Oh! I didn't realize that,' I murmured, wandering across to look at the model of Megan Price. She was very pretty, with a tip-tilted nose and a heart-shaped face.

'Is she your girlfriend?' I asked.

He nodded. 'Heaven knows what she sees in a struggling sculptor,' he smiled. 'Especially when half the men in the county are after her.'

'She's lovely,' I said.

'Yes. She has jet black hair and blue eyes. But there's a snag. She's far too rich for me. Still – mustn't bore you with my problems.'

'Why not? I've bored you with mine.'

'Your problems can be solved,' he said. 'Mine can't.'

That evening I packed all I'd need for the weekend, except the dress I was going to wear for Susan's party, because I didn't want it to get creased. I held it in front of me, looking at my reflection in the long mirror, trying to imagine Mike's expression when he saw me in it.

Helen and I had tramped around the West End for ages before we found it. 'Has it absolutely *got* to be royal blue?' she was complaining, just before we discovered it, in Selfridges. The colour was what mattered most. Mike said the first thing he noticed about me was that I had very unusual deep blue eyes. Once, when I was wearing a royal blue silk scarf, he'd held it against my face and said, 'This is the exact colour of your eyes, Lorna. It makes your hair shine gold, too.'

So I'd bought mascara, and started using eye shadow.

The dress was quite simple, off the shoulders, with a deep frill bordering the top. The material was soft and silky, with a faint sheen, and I thought the colour really did make my hair look more golden, as Mike had said. It's just ordinary fair hair, not really blonde, but when it's first washed, it does shine gold. I wear it long, so I can do things with it if I feel like it.

I stared at my face in the mirror, wondering why Peter wanted to model me. I've always thought my mouth was too wide. Still, Mike thought I was pretty, and that was all that mattered.

I hung the dress back in the wardrobe. I'd bought it to wear for Mike's seventeenth birthday party, which, in the end, didn't happen. His parents said he could either have a big party, or a car, and he chose the car, so I'd been saving the dress for some other occasion, never dreaming that there wouldn't *be* a suitable occasion, because soon I'd be hundreds of miles away from Mike.

I put on the record, 'Flip side of Loving', and listened to it as I undressed, moving to the music, and I suddenly realized that tonight might be my last night in this room, in this bed, in this house!

Not that it would be easy to find somewhere to live. I knew that. But Mike would help me. After all, it was his suggestion. I took his letter out from underneath my pillow and read it again as the record ended.

Then I slid into bed and gazed at his photo. 'Tomorrow,' I whispered, 'we'll be together again, and everything will be perfect.'

Chapter 3

I woke early next morning, feeling great. Dad drove me to the station, and soon I was on the train, too excited to read the magazines I'd bought.

Helen and Susan were waiting for me as the train drew in to Paddington. Both were wearing velour tracksuits with polo collars. Susan's was black and made her ash-blond hair look silvery. She had a very good figure, too. Helen's track suit was light blue and suited her because she's dark, and wears her hair short and straight. She has a sort of elfin face, and when she smiles, she looks like a happy pixie.

Susan drove us to Wimbledon, and, as the car turned the corner into the road where I'd lived all my life, I felt tears prick at the back of my eyes. I leaned forward to get a glimpse of our old house as we passed it.

There were new net curtains at the windows. They'd taken out the magnolia tree from the front garden, and there was a new oak front door. So what was wrong with our old front door?

'They've redecorated right through,' Susan said. 'People usually do, don't they?'

'Are they nice?' I asked, knowing they couldn't be, because it was a lovely magnolia tree.

'Don't know,' Helen answered. 'We never see them.'

'You know what it's like around here,' Susan smiled. 'Dad travels up to town every day in the train with the same people, and doesn't know any of them.'

Not like Caeraddon, I thought, where everyone knows absolutely everything about you. It was creepy. I'd never get used to it.

Helen's mother had tea ready for us, then we went up to Helen's room which has two single beds, one of which I'd sleep in that night. As I hung up my royal blue dress, Helen said, 'Well – what have you arranged with Mike, for tonight?'

'Nothing definite,' I moaned. 'I thought I'd ring him soon. He does know I'm here today, so he might ring here.' Then I told her I hadn't been able to get in touch with him by phone from home. 'Where can he possibly go, *every evening*?' I wailed.

She frowned, then said, 'Oh I know! It'll be the sports centre. Rob did say that Mike had joined again after you left. He'll be practically living there – badminton, tennis, swimming . . .'

Rob was Helen's boyfriend, nice and friendly, with beautiful eyes – except that he wore horn-rimmed glasses, so you only noticed his eyes when he took the specs off. They'd been together for ages, but I didn't think Helen felt about Rob the way I felt about Mike.

'The sports centre?' I murmured. 'What – *every night*?'

'Well, I do know that he and Zara went there practically every night,' she said. 'Zara's mad on the physical stuff, too.' Then she added quickly, 'Not that he's seeing *her* again. I didn't mean that! She's still going around with the guy she chucked Mike for – the one with the group that's been on television.'

I was longing to hear Mike's voice. 'I'll ring him now,' I said. 'What shall I arrange for this evening?'

Helen thought for a moment. 'You and Mike will want to be on your own,' she said, 'but you know what Mum's like. Better if she thinks we're going out in a foursome. Tell Mike to come here and pick us up and we'll meet Rob at the disco. You and Mike can go off together, then we'll meet up later and come home together, as if we've all been at the disco.'

Mike answered the phone, and my heart began to race.

'Hi, stranger,' I said. 'Where've you been every evening when I've phoned?'

'I didn't know you'd phoned,' he answered. 'I've been working. Didn't Mum tell you? I've got an evening job in a café.'

'Oh!' Relief spread through me, then, anxiously, I asked, 'You're not working tonight, are you?'

'Of course not! I fixed ages ago to have tonight and tomorrow night off. If I'd known what train you were catching I'd have met you at the station.'

We arranged that he'd come and pick up Helen and me at seven thirty.

Over dinner, Helen's parents asked me about Caeraddon.

I didn't dwell on the big, rambling old house, except to say that it needed painting and Dad couldn't afford to do it yet.

'Across the road from the house,' I said, 'there's a

stretch of tussocky grass, then the cliff edge, but it's not a steep cliff. There's a path down to the beach, but you have to climb over rocks to get to the sandy part. William and Andrew spend hours messing about in the rock pools.' I paused, suddenly remembering the dog which had come alive as I touched it – the feel of the wet tongue on my hand, the smell of the sea and the whining of the wind.

'Go on, Lorna,' Helen's father prompted. 'What about the village?'

'Small,' I said, 'with funny little shops either side of the main street which goes up a steep hill with the church at the top. Mum and Dad know lots of people, already. The local people are very friendly, always dropping in.' I thought, That's when I go up to my room and play my cassettes. I suppose, really, it's embarrassing for Mum and Dad. Selfish and anti-social.

Mr and Mrs Barton were nodding encouragingly, so I gathered my wandering thoughts and went on, 'The rooms in the house are so big that our furniture looks smaller than it did here, at number 30. We've got to get new carpets, but they'll have to wait because the curtains didn't fit the big windows, and we had to have new ones made.'

'It all sounds lovely, Lorna,' Mrs Barton said. 'I can't think why you don't like it. It's just the sort of place that Harry and I would like to retire to – isn't it Harry?'

Mr Barton agreed, and Helen muttered, 'Well Lorna isn't quite ready to retire, Mum. She wants to live a bit, first.'

I didn't want to be caught looking at the clock on the mantelpiece, so I kept stealing glances at my watch, hoping no one noticed, wishing time would fly, so I could be with Mike.

At last, Helen and I were ready and waiting. I wore my black shiny pants with my new emerald green top, and my heart was pounding as we raced down the stairs when the doorbell rang.

Mrs Barton reminded us to take cardigans because it would be chilly, later.

Helen opened the door, and there was Mike, smiling at me as if we'd only parted yesterday, and I could hardly speak as I gazed at him. He seemed taller, stronger, the thick hair even fairer, and his skin tanned golden.

We dropped Helen off at the disco where Rob was waiting, and promised to pick them both up at half past ten, then Mike drove on towards the common.

He talked about his job. 'General dogsbody,' he laughed, 'that's me! I prepare vegetables, sweep the floor, wash up. I need the money for the car. I can do the repairs myself, but the parts cost a fortune, and Dad says I'll take more care of the car if I have to work to keep it. By the way, I'm free all Sunday, so I can take you to the station.'

'But,' I murmured, 'I'm not sure about going back on Sunday. You know what I said in my letter, about your idea that I could leave school, and live here again?'

'Oh – well, I thought you meant later on, when we'd had a chance to see what jobs there were around here – if any.'

'How could I get a job here if I was in Wales?' I demanded. 'Anyway, I've been thinking seriously about it, and on the way here in the train, I worked out that I've enough money to last a few weeks. Gran keeps putting money into my saving account for birthdays and Christmas.'

He drove on to the common, parked the car, and turned and took me in his arms and kissed me. I put my arms around his neck and thought I'd die of happiness.

It was a lovely warm evening, left over from summer, and we wandered hand in hand across the common, as we had on our last night together. Oh – *surely* we didn't have to part again? I just couldn't bear it!

'Don't you want me to come back?' I asked in a small voice, dreading the answer, because he didn't seem to want to talk about it.

'Of course I do!' He squeezed my hand as he said it, 'but – well, it's not easy, is it? The cost of renting even a bed-sitter . . . A guy I work with at the café is giving up his bed-sitter because he can't afford it. He's a student, and he's going to share a flat with three other students.'

'Mike!' I gasped. 'Didn't you ask him if I could take the room?'

'Well, no. It's so expensive. I never thought—'

'You just don't *care*, do you?' I snatched my hand from his and we stopped walking. I glared at him. 'You don't really want me to come back!' I accused.

'Lorna!' he sighed. 'What have I done? He hasn't moved out yet – officially. We could go and look at the room tomorrow, unless it's spoken for. But it might cost forty or fifty pounds a week, then there's gas and electricity, and you'd have to buy food and clothes, and—'

'All that money for *one room*?' I gasped.

'Probably,' he nodded. 'It's in a house where all the rooms are bed-sitters, and everyone shares the bathroom.'

'You've been there?'

He nodded. 'I pick him up on the way to work. He's a student at the Poly, working evenings in the café, like me.'

'What's the room like?'

'Nothing special. Just a room. If you're sure about staying here—'

'Of *course* I'm sure!' I snapped. 'Didn't you read my letter?'

He took my hand and we began to walk again.

'I thought,' he said, 'in time, you'd probably settle down in Wales.'

'Mike – I want to be with *you*! That's *all* I want. Oh, Mike, *why* didn't you write to me? It was awful, being out of touch. Didn't you miss me? I thought of you all the time – every day, every hour!'

He put his arm across my shoulders and I slipped mine around his waist as we walked on. 'I missed you very much,' he answered. 'I know I did suggest you might leave school and live away from home – but it was just something I thought of, off the top of my head. If I'd thought it all out, I'd have realized the terrible trouble it would cause.'

'Would that matter,' I asked, 'when it would mean we'd be together again?'

He smiled. 'O.K. I'll ring Nick and find out if the room's still available. If it is, we can go and look at it.'

For the rest of the evening, we just sat on the grass and talked. At least, I made Mike talk, telling me what was happening around here, bringing me up to date on the people we both knew. Caeraddon seemed very far away – another world.

Helen and I talked late into the night. She was as excited as I was about the room. 'You're so brave,' she whispered. 'When I think of telling Mum and Dad that I'd like to leave school – let alone that I'd like to leave home and get a job – I go cold all over. I'm such a coward! Hey – look at the time! We'd better get some sleep or we'll be tired for the party tomorrow.'

Next morning, I was helping with final preparations for the party when Mike phoned to say we could go and see the room and that he'd call for me at half past two.

I said to Helen, 'I don't know what to say to your mother. It seems rude to go off with Mike, but, Helen, I've just *got* to see this room.'

'Of course you have,' she agreed. 'You can say you've been asked to Mike's house, to see his parents.'

Helen's mother was so preoccupied with the things she and Susan were making for the buffet that I managed to let her think I was visiting Mike's parents without actually having to say so.

Mike turned the car off Wimbledon High Street and drove down several side streets, emerging at last into a long road busy with traffic. 'Nick's lent me his spare key,' he said. 'He's actually moved in to the flat with his friends, but all his stuff's still in the room. His rent's paid till the end of the month. He hasn't told many people about the room yet, in case he heard of a friend who wanted it. Bed-sitters are like gold dust around here.'

He stopped the car outside a house in a long terrace of identical houses, all very tall and shabby-looking, with peeling paintwork, and dingy nets at the windows.

I was tingling with excitement as we went in through the front door and stepped on to bare floor boards, then climbed the uncarpeted stairs almost to the top floor.

There was a strange smell – a mixture of cats, boiled cabbage, and kippers. As we passed various doors, I heard music and voices, and soon the sounds all merged into one unidentifiable noise.

Mike unlocked the door, and we stepped into a dark room. It was tiny. There was a divan bed, a cooker, a sink, a small table and chair, and a threadbare carpet on the floor. A battered chest of drawers stood under the narrow window, and one corner of the room was curtained off. Behind the dingy curtain was a length of wire stretched across the angle of the two walls, secured by nails, and there were several metal coat-hangers hanging on the wire, one with an old jacket dangling on it.

There was no room to move around. I edged my way to the window and looked out at the endless flow of traffic, the lines of battered old cars parked at the kerbs on either side of the road, and, opposite, identical tall, narrow houses.

The noise of the traffic, and the dull undercurrent of

sound in the house made me feel I had to raise my voice as I spoke. 'Mike! It's so noisy! And this awful smell! How much is the rent?'

'Forty-two pounds a week. You have to pay monthly, in advance,' he answered. 'It's not that noisy. You've just got used to the quiet of the countryside, I expect. You'll soon not notice it.'

I felt a shudder ripple down my spine. Could I really get used to this? Why not? Nick had lived here for a year. He had only moved out because he couldn't afford the rent. I looked at the array of dented sauce-pans hanging from hooks above the cooker. Nick had done his best to keep the room clean and tidy, but the cooker was old and chipped, with a piece of wire holding the door shut, and the plastic sink was stained.

I couldn't help thinking of my bedroom at Caerad-don; the white walls, the high ceiling, the wide windows where I could look out at the changing colours of sea and sky, where the only sound was the calling of the gulls. My room smelled of the lavender furniture spray polish Mum used on my chest of drawers and dressing table.

'Nick's been trying for a whole year to find some-thing cheaper,' Mike said. 'It's hopeless. You won't find anything else. What do you think of it?'

'Let's look at the bathroom,' I said, anxious to get out of the room.

The bathroom was at the end of the landing. It had bare floorboards and a bath on iron legs, with a weird-looking heater over it, which you had to put money into to get hot water.

'Oh – excuse me! Are you next?' I turned to see a tall

girl carrying a towel and shampoo and a change of clothing.

'No. We don't live here,' I answered. 'We're – just looking around.'

'Oh, good!' she sighed. 'Thought I'd missed my chance. Sometimes you can wait all day for a bath – keep on popping up and hoping to find it empty. You moving in?'

'Er – I'm not sure,' I said. 'It's expensive, and I haven't got a job yet.'

'Oh, neither have I,' she replied. 'You just left school?'

I nodded. It wasn't worth explaining.

'What you do,' she said, 'is go to the D.H.S.S. office. Tell 'em you've got a room, see? If you've got no job, they pay the rent for you and give you what other money you're due to. I don't know how much you'll get. It's different for me because I've had a job for three years. They'll explain everything.'

'They pay the rent?' I gasped. 'What – *all* of it?'

'Sure. You take proof that you've got a place to live, and they sort it out. Then you go to the Job Centre and waste your time looking for work. Anyway, I got to get on with my bath before there's a queue and they start banging on the door for me to hurry up. I'm downstairs in number five. Drop in if you take the room. You a friend of Nick's?'

Again, I nodded.

'Tell him Sharon says we miss him,' she smiled. 'See you around maybe.'

The bathroom door closed and Mike and I walked

down the stairs. In the street, I took a long deep breath. Could I really get used to that smell?

Mike drove out into the line of traffic. 'You hated it, didn't you?' he asked.

I nodded miserably. 'Didn't you hate it, too?'

'No. It's O.K. Lots of people would be glad of it. Someone will snap it up.'

'Is it true that the Social Security people pay the rent?' I asked.

'I expect so,' he answered. 'People have to live somewhere, don't they?'

'Do you want me to take the room?' I asked quietly.

'It's up to you,' he said. 'There's no choice. It's that or nothing, isn't it? And it's sheer luck you have a chance of it.'

I looked at him, anxiously. He stared straight ahead, concentrating on driving. I felt a sudden chill. If he really wanted me here, surely he'd have understood how I felt about the room, and been sympathetic? It wasn't entirely my decision – not if he wanted me to stay. There was something different about him. Maybe I was losing him!

For some time we didn't talk as he negotiated the thick traffic, and I was wrapped in misery. As we came back to Wimbledon High Street, he murmured, 'Penny for them? Are you trying to make up your mind about the room?'

'Yes,' I answered. 'I've got to work things out.'

It wasn't true. At that moment, I wasn't capable of working anything out. I was seized with a dreadful panic. I couldn't lose Mike! If he was drifting away from me, I had to get him back. I'd think about the room later.

'You'll come to the party early, won't you?' I said. 'It's going to be really great!'

'I'll be there at eight,' he promised. 'I've been looking forward to it. Having an evening job, I don't get to parties any more.'

'I've promised to go back and help with last minute jobs,' I told him. 'I'll think about the room and maybe we can discuss it tonight.'

'Right,' he nodded.

As I went into the Barton's house, Helen grabbed me in the hall. 'Roger's here,' she whispered. 'I've told him we want to ask him something that's secret, and legal.'

Susan's boyfriend, Roger, was talking to Helen's father. There didn't seem to be anything left to do for the party. Mrs Barton was in the living room, reading a magazine. 'Thanks for all your help this morning, Lorna,' she smiled. 'It made a lot of difference to get a good start.'

Roger saw me and called, 'Hi, Lorna! How are things in darkest Wales?'

'Dark,' I answered grimly. 'And boring.'

'Come outside!' Helen hissed at him, and he stepped into the hall where she pushed him towards the kitchen.

'I hope I can answer what it is you want to know,' he murmured. 'I've got several more exams before I become a legal eagle, you know.'

Helen closed the kitchen door and asked him the question. He stared at her. 'Surely not *you*, Helen?' he gasped.

'No, No! A friend,' she snapped. 'Quick, Roger, before someone comes. Can parents *do* anything?'

'Not legally, no,' he answered. 'But do tell your friend to think carefully. All the wasted opportunities for the sake of two more years at school, when she'd be eighteen, and able to leave anyway, go to college, or take up some sort of training. Why is she thinking of doing this? Trouble at home?'

'No. Er, well,' Helen spluttered, 'she made Lorna and me promise we'd tell no one any details, you see.'

Roger said, 'I wouldn't have liked to be on my own at sixteen. Tell your friend to take her time, not rush into anything. It can be very lonely out there, you know.'

'We'll tell her,' Helen promised. 'Thanks, Roger.'

We raced upstairs to Helen's room. 'So that's one problem solved,' she said. 'What's the room like?'

I sat on the bed and began to describe it, and if I hadn't felt so crushed with disappointment, I'd have had to laugh at her face, all screwed up in distaste, her expression becoming more and more horrified as I went on to describe the bathroom, and how one had to take one's turn and possibly wait for hours for a bath.

'Owch!' she said at last. 'Well, you can't live *there*!'

'Mike says I'd get used to it,' I replied. 'And Nick's lived there, and I expect the other people are as nice as the girl we met. If they can live there, why can't I?'

'Because you don't have to,' she answered. 'They've got to. And they're older than you. It's different when you're older.'

'But — I can't stand being parted from Mike,' I said. 'Helen — if you were separated from Rob, would you

47

leave home to be with him?'

'No way!' she gasped. 'I mean, Rob's terrific, and I like him a lot, but I'm not potty about him, like you are about Mike. Oh – I don't blame you,' she added quickly. 'When I saw Mike on that stage, as Hamlet, with a pool of light on him, and his face turned up, all sort of – noble, I fancied him myself for a bit. Rob's lovely, but I could live without him if I had to.'

'But – you said it would be good if we could get a flat together,' I reminded her.

'Well, leaving school is my idea of heaven, and close to that is being able to do exactly as I like – never having to say where I'm going or what time I'll be home. Rob doesn't come into it. I don't think of him as, sort of, permanent.'

I sighed. 'And you don't have to live in Caeraddon, and go to a frowsty old Grammar school, and not have any friends and have absolutely nowhere to go.'

'I know,' she answered quietly. 'I'm sorry Lorn. But that room sounds the pits, and Caeraddon's not for ever, is it? You'll leave anyway when you're eighteen, for university or somewhere.'

'That's *two years*!' I gasped. 'I'd lose him, wouldn't I? Besides, I couldn't imagine two whole years without Mike!'

She gazed at me, puzzled. 'I've never felt like that about a boy,' she said. 'What's it like?'

'Terrible when you're apart,' I sighed. 'You can't stop thinking about him. All the time you're thinking, "I must tell Mike about this", or, "I wish Mike could see this". You just long to be with him and talk to him, about absolutely everything, and know he'll under-stand.'

Helen looked blank. 'Perhaps I'll never fall in love,' she murmured.

'Of course you will,' I insisted. 'You just haven't met the right boy yet.'

'But – it doesn't sound much fun,' she said doubt-fully. 'All that misery when you're apart!'

'But when you're together, it's *wonderful*,' I smiled. 'It makes up for everything. You feel so – so *happy*! You really do feel as if you're walking on air – as if you're as light as a feather. All the colours look brighter, and you have this amazing sort of joy, inside.'

'*Honestly*?' Helen gasped. '*Wow*!'

'Only – I didn't feel like that this afternoon,' I ad-mitted. 'Something went wrong. When you have a quarrel, even a little one, it's awful. You feel – insecure. As if everything could sort of fall apart.'

'You quarrelled about the room?' she asked.

'No. We didn't argue or anything. I just had this feeling that he was fed up with me for not making up my mind. Oh, Helen, I couldn't bear to lose Mike! I've just *got* to get him back – make him feel about me the way he used to. And I've only got this evening to do it in.'

'Well – it shouldn't be too hard, not with that dress,' she grinned. 'You could have your bath straight after tea, before Susan takes over the bathroom, and I could blow-dry your hair like I used to. And Susan's got some amazing new perfume, called "Desire". We could "borrow" just a drop of it, couldn't we?'

I looked at her, and soon we were both grinning like Cheshire cats. 'Right,' I said. 'Tonight I'll make him notice me as if he'd never seen me before!'

'And if you do go back to Wales,' Helen smiled, 'he'll be ringing up every day, not writing one stingy old letter. You don't have to decide about that room today. Tell Nick to give you a few days to think about it.'

At half past six, Helen had blow-dried my hair, and it looked really good, with soft curls framing my face, and she used some of Susan's expensive conditioning hair spray on it, which brought out the gold lights and made it shine.

'That's my contribution then,' she said. 'You do your make-up, and just before the party starts, I'll sneak in and borrow Susan's perfume.'

At eight o'clock, people started arriving for the party. Helen's mother said, 'Lorna – you look lovely! That's a very pretty dress!'

By half past eight, the house was full of people, and I was dashing around offering drinks while Helen and Rob took charge of the music until Roger was free to take over. *But where was Mike?*

He still hadn't arrived at nine o'clock, so I phoned his home. His mother said he was out. 'Gone to a party, I think,' she added. 'Oh – you're at the party? Well he set out just before eight o'clock, I think. Perhaps his car's broken down. It often does.'

I joined in the dancing and tried not to worry, but at ten o'clock, I was getting frantic. Then the doorbell rang and no one heard it above the music and laughter and chatter. No one except me.

Mike stood on the doorstep, his hands and face covered in black grease. 'Sorry,' he said. 'The car broke down. Let me get cleaned up and I'll explain what happened.'

Ten minutes later, he emerged from the bathroom, looking presentable, but with a smear of grease on the sleeve of his shirt. 'I carry overalls with me,' he said, 'but they must have come open. I don't suppose this smear is noticeable.'

Susan and Roger danced out into the hall and Susan called, 'Hi, Mike! Thought you'd been kidnapped. What happened?'

'His car broke down,' I answered.

'Bad luck,' Roger said. 'You managed to fix it?'

'Oh yes,' Mike replied. 'The fan belt broke. I found out why. It had been rubbing against the metal edge of the generator mounting which had worked loose. A nut had vibrated off the bolt holding the generator in position, you see, and—'

'Tell him the details some other time,' I interrupted, grabbing Mike's arm and giving Susan a look she understood at once.

'No talking about cars at my party,' Susan laughed. 'It's strictly forbidden. Lorna, take Mike to the buffet, and we must keep him and Roger apart!'

Helen's father passed us in the doorway and said, 'Ah, Mike! Lorna was worried about you. What happened?'

This time I couldn't stop Mike in time, and Mr Barton seemed quite interested to hear how Mike had found a nut of the right size holding the horn unit in position, and had decided the horn unit could do with

51

one less nut so that he could effect his repair.

I danced with Rob while Helen danced with one of Roger's friends.

'Are you interested in cars?' I asked Rob.

'I don't know much about how they work,' he said, 'but I'm very interested in being seventeen in one month's time and passing my driving test. I suppose I'll have to learn how to do repairs, then.'

'Ask Mike,' I muttered darkly. 'He'll teach you.'

He laughed. 'Mike's a brilliant mechanic,' he said.

I wondered why I was so angry. Mike couldn't help his car breaking down. I suppose it was because I'd worried so much, for nothing. I'd imagined him in a road accident. Then I'd thought he'd decided not to come, and never to see me again. Now he was here, at last, and all he could do was talk about the wretched car! And I had only this evening to do all in my power to convince him that I was the only girl for him! Time was passing. I couldn't afford to be angry.

When I looked around for Mike, I couldn't find him, and eventually discovered him in the kitchen, talking to Mrs Barton. 'Just coming, Lorna,' he said, and turned back to Mrs Barton. 'What I meant was,' he told her, 'you can always improvise a fan belt, if it breaks, so long as you have something like a pair of nylong tights. I once drove all the way back from Brighton with a pair of tights acting as a fan belt.'

Mrs Barton was wearing a polite but glazed expression as I dragged Mike away.

As we danced, I guided him towards the open French windows. Then I said, quietly, 'Whose tights did you get back from Brighton with?'

He blinked. 'Oh — they were Zara's. She wasn't exactly pleased, but all the garages were shut, so—'

'When was this?'

'*When*? Ages ago. Why?'

'When you were going around with Zara Harrison, you didn't have a car,' I reminded him. 'You got it for your seventeenth birthday, after you broke with Zara.'

He looked blank for a moment, then said, 'It must have been a car I borrowed, then.'

I stopped dancing, a chill settling on my chest.

'Let's go outside,' I murmured.

The garden looked lovely, with fairy lights in the trees. The evening was warm, filled with the scent of honeysuckle that grew against the house wall.

It was quiet outside, and my voice sounded icy as I said, 'You couldn't have borrowed a car before you were seventeen, because you didn't have a licence, and you've been going out with me since one month before your seventeenth birthday.'

We walked away from the house, towards the vegetable plot. 'O.K.,' Mike sighed. 'After you left, I took Zara out once or twice. It was still the holidays, with nothing to do.'

'You went back to Zara, and didn't even bother to tell me,' I choked, trying to keep the sob out of my voice.

'There was nothing to tell,' he insisted. 'Besides, your letters were so — well — possessive, that I could hardly write back and say I'd been seeing Zara now and again.'

'Is *that* why you didn't write to me?'

'I did write.'

'Once! *One* letter!'

'Well, with this evening job, there isn't much time. And I knew you were coming back for this party, didn't I?'

'So it wasn't worth bothering to keep in touch?'

'No — I didn't mean that!' He sighed deeply. 'Look, Lorna,' he said, 'this is getting altogether too heavy for me. You see, Zara doesn't make demands on a guy. You know what I mean?'

We were standing by Mr Barton's runner beans, out of sight of the house now, and quite alone. The scent of the beans was sweet and fresh. I looked up at Mike in the half-light, unable to see the expression on his face. 'No,' I replied. 'I don't know what you mean. I thought you and Zara were finished. You said you loved *me*. You *did*!'

'I did love you, Lorna. I — I *do*. You're the prettiest girl I've ever known, and you're good fun — great to be with. Only, when I put in my letter about how you could come back and get a job in London — it was just to cheer you up.'

'*What*?' I gasped.

'It was — the sort of thing you say. I mean, if I was really fed up at home, I suppose I'd think about getting out, and living somewhere else.'

'But — the only reason I thought about it seriously was so we could be together,' I whispered.

He put his hands on my arms, gently, and stood looking down at me. 'We had something special, Lorna,' he said softly. 'Something really good together. But, like I said, it got too heavy. I guess I'm not really into deep relationships yet.'

'But — you took me to see the room. What if I'd decided to take it?'

'What do you mean?'

'You'd have let me take a big step like that, when you don't really care if I'm here or not!'

'What? Of *course* I care! I wish you hadn't had to go away. I wouldn't have gone out with Zara if you'd still been here.'

I drew away from him, trying to work out exactly what he was saying.

He caught my arms and pulled me back, close to him. 'If you want to take that room,' he said, 'I'll help you all I can. I mean, we're good friends, aren't we? I wouldn't let you down.'

He drew me into his arms, and all I wanted was to be close to him, to be warm and safe and protected and loved. He kissed me gently, and I closed my eyes, letting the peace of the garden enclose us. Then, suddenly, I felt my body stiffen, and drew away from him.

'What's wrong now?' He sounded mystified.

'Everything!' I choked, and ran back into the house, up to Helen's room, where I closed the door and flung myself on the bed sobbing.

By the time Helen came looking for me, I'd managed to control myself, and washed my face, so that no one would know — but Helen knew straight away.

'What's happened?' she demanded. 'It's past two o'clock, and everyone's leaving, but Susan says Mike left ages ago. You and Mike have had a row, haven't you?'

I nodded. 'Tell you in the morning. I'm too tired to talk now.'

'O.K.,' she nodded. 'Super party, wasn't it?'

'Yes — really super,' I agreed. We both began to undress. I didn't bother to hang the royal blue dress in the wardrobe. I pushed it into my suitcase without even folding it. Mike had been too busy talking about fan belts to notice it.

'It's that bed-sitter, isn't it?' Helen muttered. 'Lorn — I've had another idea, but it's a chance in a million. If your parents would let you live here, with us, you could go back to our school for "A" levels. I'm pretty sure Mum and Dad would agree, because I know they like you a lot. But I don't suppose your parents would consider it. They wouldn't be able to understand — about Mike, I mean. Still, I thought I'd mention it — just in case . . . '

She pulled on her nightdress, and was about to climb into bed. I looked at her, and tears came back into my eyes and brimmed over.

'Hey,' she murmured. 'I'm sorry, Lorn. I was only trying to think of every possibility.'

I flung my arms around her and we clung together.

'Oh, Helen,' I choked, 'you're the best friend anyone could ever have! Mum and Dad would never agree, and anyway, it's all different now. But thanks!'

Helen was soon asleep, but I lay awake, staring up at the ceiling. We'd forgotten to close the curtains, and moonlight streamed in through the window.

Mike didn't love me. I'd have done anything for him; even lived in that grotty room to be near him, to be able to see him every day. I might as well admit now that I'd been deliberately hiding the truth from myself.

I'd told myself that boys aren't emotional, like girls are, and that letter-writing and phoning seemed a waste of time to them, but it didn't mean they felt differently, deep down.

If I hadn't overheard Mike talking to Mrs Barton, I wouldn't have known that he'd taken Zara to Brighton, and then we wouldn't have had that conversation by the runner beans, and I might have gone on deceiving myself, making myself believe that Mike loved me.

Now I knew the truth. I could still have Mike as a boyfriend if I remembered that he wasn't into deep relationships. And if I didn't mind sharing him with Zara.

He couldn't possibly have understood what leaving home would have meant to me. I didn't mind at all leaving Caeraddon, but during the time since Mike's letter had arrived, I'd had a few glimpses of what life would be like without my family. When Dad gave me a quick hug at bedtime, I'd thought, "It'll be awful, leaving Dad". I'd looked at Andrew, absorbed in making a model of a ship at the kitchen table, his eyes screwed up in concentration, and I'd thought, "He's a great nuisance, sometimes, but I'll miss him". I suppose a baby brother always stays special, even when he's no longer a baby.

I hadn't dared think about what it would be like not having Mum to turn to when things went wrong, or to discuss things like clothes with. I'd just shut that out of my mind. Although I couldn't help the way I'd behaved since we went to Wales, I'd felt guilty about it. I knew she was being extra patient with me, thinking I needed time to settle down.

Since we went to Caeraddon, I'd been surprised to find that William wasn't just a kid any more – well, not all the time. Sometimes, we'd discussed things I'd never have dreamed of talking to him about only a year ago. He's got a way of looking at things differently that's interesting – maybe it's because he's artistic.

It would be quite different, leaving home to go to college, knowing I could come back for vacations – knowing they'd all still be there.

Seeing that room had shattered the dream I'd had, so briefly, of being free and independent, making my own decisions about everything. Yet, if Mike had really loved me, and wanted me to come back here, I suppose I'd have gone right ahead and made the break. I just couldn't be sure.

I closed my eyes. It was all too mixed up – too difficult to understand. Tomorrow, I'd talk it all over with Helen, and try to make sense of everything.

Chapter 4

Suddenly it was morning, and Helen was putting a cup of tea on the bedside table.

'It's ten o'clock,' she said. 'I let you lie in.'

'Oh no!' I groaned. 'I ought to be up and helping to clear up after the party!'

'Don't worry,' she smiled. 'We all got up late. There's still plenty of work to do. We've not had breakfast yet anyway.'

I was glad to be rushing around with the vacuum cleaner, helping to restore order. It left me no time to think. When I went to tell Mr Barton that lunch would soon be ready, I felt practically human again. He got up to switch off the video recording he was watching, and I said, 'No – don't switch it off yet. Lunch will be at least ten minutes. What are you watching?'

'Just something that was on television last night, during the party,' he said. 'It's an arts programme I usually watch, so I taped it.'

I glanced at the screen, and nearly dropped the plates I was carrying into the dining room. 'Mr Barton!' I squeaked. 'I know that man! He lives in Caeraddon!'

I couldn't believe it! It was Peter Jackson, sitting in the studio where I'd sat only two days ago. 'I didn't know he was famous!' I gasped.

'I don't suppose he is,' Mr Barton smiled. 'He's on this programme because he's won some sort of award. I'll wind it back so you can see it all.'

'Let me get Helen,' I said. 'I've told her about him. I can't believe this! He never said he was going to be on television on Saturday night!'

'Oh, this would be recorded months ago,' Mr Barton said. 'They didn't say it was Caeraddon, or I'd have fetched you, to see it. They just said South Wales.'

Soon, the whole family and I were sitting close to the

television set, avidly watching.

The programme began with a view of the coastline, and the narrator saying 'This surprisingly unspoilt stretch of the Welsh coastline is where Peter Jackson, winner of the Blakestone award, lives and works. The award is offered annually for the best piece of representational sculpture.'

Then there was Peter, in his car, with Jack beside him, driving down from the village, and talking. 'That's our house!' I shrieked, as he drove past it, saying, 'I could make a long list of reasons why I chose to live in this area. One – I could afford it – almost. Two, I had happy holidays here as a child, with an aunt who lived in the village. Three, I like the people. There are countless more reasons. For an artist, working in any medium, such a quiet, beautiful place as this has everything to offer.'

He got out of the car, and he and Jack went into the studio. The interviewer appeared, and sat where I'd sat only the other day. I felt as if I couldn't breathe in case I missed anything!

On the table between Peter and the interviewer was a model, about a foot high, of the group I'd seen, life-size. 'This,' Peter said, indicating it, 'is the maquette which I entered for the competition.'

'What's a maquette?' Helen whispered.

'Sh!' Susan hissed, and then the camera roamed over the shelves, showing other pieces of Peter's work, without a commentary, so Mr Barton muttered, 'A maquette is a small model of something that's going to be made.'

'The group,' Peter said, 'Will be life-size.' He went

on to talk about the local foundry where it would be cast in bronze, then pictures were shown of his other work, like a bronze of a girl dancing, that was on permanent exhibition somewhere in France, and a man throwing a discus that was in a park somewhere in Scotland.

When the programme was over, Susan said, 'He's really something! I expect he's got a girlfriend?'

'He has,' I grinned, 'and what about poor Roger?'

She laughed. 'A trainee solicitor doesn't seem very romantic, compared with a sculptor in a lonely cottage by the sea. On the other hand, that man is far too good-looking to feel safe with!'

'Who wants to feel *safe*?' Helen giggled. 'That dog is the one you rescued, isn't it, Lorn?'

So then I had to repeat the story about Jack, to explain how I knew Peter.

Mr Barton wound the tape back and put it on "pause", so we could look at our house.

'It's absolutely *lovely*!' Mrs Barton exclaimed. 'Lorna, you *naughty* girl, not to tell us how large it was! Those beautiful big windows, all looking out to sea! And the front garden full of roses!'

'You can have the tape to take home,' Mr Barton said. 'I wasn't going to keep it anyway, and your parents will want to see it.'

I tried to insist on paying for it, but he just laughed and rewound the tape and put it into its box and gave it to me. 'I'm sure Dad will send you a new tape in exchange,' I said, embarrassed, but delighted to have the tape.

After lunch, he got the car out to take me to the

station. Helen came too, and we sat in the back seat. I'd told her what had happened between me and Mike as I flung things into my suitcase. 'Shouldn't you phone him, before you go?' she asked anxiously. 'To – sort of clear things up. Make sure you've done the right thing?'

I shook my head decisively. 'Things *are* cleared up,' I answered.

I told her that the spare room would be ready by half term if she wanted to come and stay with us.

'I'm *dying* to come,' she said.

As the train drew out of the station, and I waved to Mr Barton and Helen, I thought, 'This time, it really *is* goodbye to London. I've got to stop thinking of it as home.'

That morning, I'd awakened with a feeling of something being terribly wrong – of some awful sadness waiting to loom up on me. As I drank the tea Helen had brought me, the cold misery began to descend, spreading right through me. Then, suddenly, it wasn't sadness that was washing over me. It was anger. I was mad at myself more than at Mike. For a whole month, I'd thought only of him. When I wasn't writing a letter to him, I was composing one in my mind, or planning what I'd say to him when we met again, remembering things he'd said to me, and how he'd looked when he'd said them. Nothing I saw, or did, in Caeraddon was real. I was simply existing until I saw Mike again, and came alive.

The worst thing of all was that I actually *knew*, inside myself, all the time, that Mike didn't love me. I knew, because of course he'd have phoned, or written oftener, or even driven down to see me.

So – O.K., I was wrong not to face facts. It didn't help at all to realize that, but it set me free to think about Mike.

I couldn't forgive him for going out with Zara Harrison. How smug she must feel, to know that, having dropped Mike for someone she liked better, she could have him back at any time. I was no obstacle to her.

By the time I'd finished the tea, I was furious. Later, as I shoved the vacuum cleaner around, watching it snap up crumbs, listening to its horrible noise, it was Mike I was angry with, more than myself.

I didn't need him. And I would never, *never* again, let myself fall in love with a boy. From now on, I'd keep my cool so well I'd be made of ice. No boy would ever hurt me again. An all-girls school would suit me fine! Gwenally Grammar, I thought, here I come!

When I'd watched the video with Helen's family, I was seeing Caeraddon properly for the first time. I'd trudged up that hill to the village, hating the place, because it separated me from Mike. And he wasn't worth it. No boy was worth it!

I gazed dully out of the carriage window. Grimy brick walls with peeling posters. Scruffy narrow streets with shops and hairdresser's all closed, because it was Sunday. Soon we were hurrying through suburbia – neat gardens and trees in the streets. Then London was gone.

I didn't feel angry or sad any more. I just felt numb. The train wound on through lush green countryside, where the trees were showing the first autumn tints of gold.

It didn't matter how long the journey took, I thought. I might as well be sitting on a train as doing anything else. There was nothing to think about, nothing to plan, nothing to look forward to.

I closed my eyes, and woke up with a jerk as the train drew in to the station where I had to change for Gwenally. Very soon, I was leaning out of the carriage window at Gwenally station, searching the platform for Dad, suddenly longing to see him. I wanted to fling my arms around him and feel him lift me off my feet in a bear-hug, the way we always greeted each other.

Dad wasn't there. I dumped my case on the platform. It wasn't like Dad to be late. I felt tears pricking at my eyes. This was stupid, and I pulled myself together. I'd find a phone and see what had happened. I could easily get a taxi home.

A voice behind me panted, 'Hi, Lorna!' I turned to see Gwillym Evans smiling at me. 'Sorry I'm late. Your Dad's got trouble with his car so I offered to come and meet you.'

'Oh – thanks,' I said, without enthusiasm. It was Dad I wanted to see. Dad I needed, not Gwillym Evans.

'What's wrong with the car?' I muttered as he picked up my case and we set off towards the exit.

'It wouldn't start,' he said. 'Then when it did, it packed up again outside our front gate. I went to see if I could help. Your Dad was getting anxious about being late to meet you, so I offered, and my Dad said I could take the Land Rover – it's faster than my old crate.'

It seemed as if cars had something against me this weekend; first Mike's, then Dad's. And it was almost as if Mum had planned this, except that I couldn't quite see her sabotaging the car to throw Gwillym and me together.

'Was it a good weekend?' he asked as we drove towards the coast road.

'Er – on the whole, I suppose so,' I answered, unprepared for the question.

He glanced at me briefly. 'Reservations?'

I laughed. 'Parts of the weekend were very good.'

'And you're trying to forget the other parts?'

'Right!' I grinned.

'Let's change the subject then,' he smiled.

He told me that Jack was making a very good recovery and was now home with Peter again. I told him about seeing Peter on television.

'That was shown on TV here about five weeks ago,' he said. 'Caeraddon's moment of fame.'

He'd finished working on the farm, and was having a few days' break before starting at Art School. 'This is the first time I've ever wanted a holiday to pass quickly,' he said. 'Are you looking forward to starting at the Grammar school?'

'No, I can't say I'm counting the days,' I replied. 'In fact, I'd like the holiday to go on for ever.'

'I know one or two girls who'll be in the sixth forms at Gwenally Grammar next term. Would you like to meet them?'

'No, thanks,' I said quickly. 'I'd rather go in at the deep end.'

He nodded. 'I think I would, too. Better to choose your friends than have them thrust upon you.'

I agreed, but the truth was that I didn't want anyone feeling they had to be nice to me, out of duty, and I didn't care about starting at a new school any more. I didn't care about anything.

'What do you think of the village?' he asked, 'now that you've been here long enough to get the feel of the place?'

'It's – er – well, very pretty. Quaint and old-fashioned. The countryside around here is really lovely,' I murmured.

He laughed softly, and I looked at his profile in surprise. He really was, as Mum kept saying, very good looking. The dark eyes had thick lashes that any girl would envy – including me.

'Sorry to laugh,' he said. 'You can't bring yourself, out of politeness to a native, to say you hate the place. But I understand. How can anyone settle easily here, after London?'

'Peter did,' I said. 'And he told me that your father worked in a London veterinary practice for a time.'

'Oh – Dad never left Wales at all, not in his heart,' he smiled. 'While he was working in the Chelsea practice he probably wore a daffodil in his buttonhole all the time! He'd never settle anywhere permanently, except in Wales.'

'And are you madly patriotic about Wales, too?' I asked.

'Oh yes, I think so,' he grinned. 'I expect there's a red dragon tattooed on my heart.'

'I don't hate this place,' I said quietly. 'It's just such a complete change from London. It seems dull, with nothing to do.'

'Not a lot happening,' he agreed. 'But Gwenally is pretty lively.'

'*Lively*?' I repeated.

'If you don't compare it with New York, of course,' he said. 'There's discos, and a repertory theatre, and cinema. There's a really good folk club I go to quite often, on Monday evenings. Fancy coming with me tomorrow?'

I wasn't expecting it, and caught my breath. 'Well – thanks, but I – er . . . '

'You've got a boyfriend in London, and he'd go spare?'

'No,' I answered. 'I've tied up all my loose ends in London.'

Gwillym turned the car into the road that led down through the village. 'It's O.K.,' he said quietly. 'I don't ask twice.'

'Oh, Gwillym, I'm sorry,' I gasped. 'I didn't get much sleep this weekend, and I'm sort of – woolly. I would like to go with you to the folk club. Thank you for asking me.'

He glanced at me quickly. 'You're sure? No need to be polite just because we're neighbours.'

'No, I told you. I'm half asleep really.'

'We could go somewhere else, if you like. There's a disco on Mondays, too. Maybe you don't like folk music.'

'I love it,' I answered firmly.

'Well then you won't be disappointed. You can't beat Wales for music, you know.'

'I know,' I nodded.

It was very odd, but suddenly, I wanted very much to go with him. Maybe it was the way he said, 'I don't ask twice'. With Gwillym, you knew exactly where you were.

Once in our house, I got my bear-hug from Dad. As he lifted me off my feet, he said, 'Sorry about the car, love. Come and tell us all about the weekend.'

'The new people in our house have dug up the magnolia tree,' I told him.

'What? Well, I wish I'd known they didn't want it. I could have brought it here.'

Andrew flung his arms around my waist, looking up at me. 'I needed you, yesterday,' he said accusingly. 'Mr Jones found the kite for me, in his attic, and it's super, but it's old and won't fly, because it needs mending.'

Mum hugged me and said I looked tired.

William rushed through the door shouting, 'Hi, Lorna! How's the great lover of Wimbledon?'

'I can't think whom you mean,' I said, in a snooty, upper class voice.

'The guy with the wheels,' he grinned. 'Mister Mike, the Motor Car.'

'Oh – *him*!' I nodded. 'Still going at a steady sixty miles an hour.'

But not with me, I thought. Not any more.

Dad was muttering to William about how impolite it was to criticize people. 'You'll be just the same when you get your first car,' he said, 'and it's good for a boy to be really enthusiastic about something.'

Funny, I thought, I'd never realized that Mike was obsessed with cars before this weekend, yet it was obvious to everyone else – even to William! I'd been living in a world where Mike was what I wanted him to be, and nothing he did was boring or tiresome.

Andrew raced off to get the kite – an elaborate affair made of red nylon attached to thin strips of wood. 'It's a box kite,' he explained. 'But it won't fly until the cloth is sewn back on.'

'I offered to do it,' Mum said, 'but he insisted it was your job.'

'Lorna mended my model battleship, and my roller skate,' Andrew said. 'She's great at fixing things.'

Mum smiled. 'I know I'm not in her class when it comes to battleships and roller skates,' she said. 'But I *can* sew! I shall now go away and sulk.'

Andrew giggled, and I picked up the kite. It was a simple job to rejoin the seams that had come apart. He fetched Mum's sewing box and put it on the kitchen table. 'Hey – don't I get time for a cup of tea, first?' I protested.

'I want to fly it,' he begged. 'I've been waiting and *waiting* for you to come home!'

I looked down at the tousled fair hair, and the dark blue eyes gazing at me imploringly. He'd been waiting for me to come home. Would I ever be able to think of this house as home?

'You go and make me a cup of tea, then,' I said. 'I'll start on this now.'

Chapter 5

There was something very different about the Sunday evening at home at the end of that awful weekend. One of Mum's new friends dropped in, Mrs Thomas, who is the district nurse. Normally, this would have been my cue to go upstairs and sit in my room listening to music, but Mrs Thomas was so friendly and cheerful that I stayed and listened to stories about her patients. She had us in fits of laughter, describing hilarious things that had happened on her rounds.

I'd often thought about nursing as a career. I asked Mrs Thomas what it was like, being a probationer nurse in a hospital, and again, she had us all laughing as she recalled her training, in a big London hospital. What she told us was interesting, too, and when she left I realized that my preoccupation with the misery of parting with Mike had been pushed into the background for a time.

Just as I was going to bed, Dad whispered to me to come into the kitchen, and I followed him, mystified.

He shut the door. 'Lorna,' he said, 'I need your help. I want to get Mum something nice for our wedding anniversary in two weeks' time. Jewellery of some kind. You know the sort of thing she likes better than I do. Will you come and help me choose something?'

'Oh Dad!' I gasped excitedly. 'When? What are you

going to buy — a locket or bracelet or something?'

'Whatever you think she'd like,' he answered. 'But I'm going to spend quite a lot of money, so I want to be sure she'll like it. This anniversary is special, in a way, because our lives have completely changed. I want Mum to know that I appreciate how she's supported me.'

'You mean, about coming here?' I said.

He nodded. 'She hated leaving London, and having to start afresh, here,' he said, 'but she never once complained. I was so busy with the firm's removal, that I had no spare time, and she took over all the moving arrangements and made it easier for all of us to settle in here.'

I was puzzled. Mum had seemed quite enthusiastic about the move.

'There's a good jewellers' in Gwenally,' Dad went on, 'but if we can't find anything suitable there, we can go in to Cardiff or Swansea one day next week. Meantime, if you'd be thinking about what sort of thing—'

'She likes old-fashioned jewellery,' I said. 'Antique rings, lockets, pendants, and those Victorian fob-watches.'

Dad smiled. 'You see why I need your help. I'd have no idea what to choose, and I do want it to be a surprise.'

I climbed into bed, thinking about what he'd said, ashamed suddenly of the way I'd behaved since we came here. I realized now that *of course* Mum hadn't wanted to come here. She'd been involved in so many things at home, in London. There was charity work, raising funds for the local children's home. She and Dad liked going to concerts at the Barbican and the

Festival Hall. Mum went to the opera with a friend, regularly. Friends were always ringing her or calling in.

Now I could see how hard it must have been to give up the things she was so interested in, and start afresh, here.

And what had I done to help? Nothing! I'd moaned and complained, made a terrible fuss about having to change schools, refused to be sociable with people who called. I must have added to all Dad's worries as well.

I'd never once heard Mum complain, or even look unhappy, except when I'd hung about, moping, saying there was nothing to do here, nowhere to go.

I was sitting up in bed, hugging my knees, hot with shame as I recalled the various childish things I'd done and said, when the door opened, and William crept into my bedroom in his pyjamas.

'Hey!' I snapped. 'You're not supposed to come in here without knocking! Why aren't you in bed?'

'Sh!' he hissed. 'I've got to talk to you – it's important. Only first, you've got to swear to tell no-one – absolutely *no-one*.'

'Tell them what?'

'Swear!'

'How can I, when I don't know what—?'

'Oh, listen,' he sighed. 'This isn't kid's stuff.'

'What have you done?' I asked warily.

'Swear first,' he insisted.

'O.K. I swear.'

He sat on the bed and said, 'You know that logbook that Andrew keeps, with dates and times of what happens?'

72

I nodded. 'You've gone and lost it!'

'*No!*' he frowned. '*Listen!* Remember that stuff about the sailing ship that goes into the side of the cliff? Well he's got other notes about a rowing boat with two men in it, and *that* disappears into the cliff as well.'

'But it can't,' I said. 'So—'

'No, it doesn't. At least, the rowing boat doesn't. It goes into a cave. I don't know about the sailing ship. That must be an optical whatsit. You know?'

'Optical illusion,' I said.

He nodded. 'Yes. Because the sailing ship hasn't been sighted again anyway. But you see, I climbed out along the reef and watched for the rowing boat.'

'So?' I asked.

'Well, Dad told me never to go out on the reef at high tide, but that's when the rowing boat comes in, and I wanted to see where it went, because I didn't know about the cave, then. And – so I could watch it, I took Dad's field glasses.'

'William!' I gasped. 'You know how expensive those field glasses are! Dad told you never to take them outside the house without asking him.'

'That,' William muttered, 'is why I can't tell anyone but you what happened.'

I groaned. 'You'll have to own up,' I told him. 'If you've dropped those expensive field glasses into the sea—'

'But I *haven't*,' he insisted. 'Well – not exactly. I mean – I can get them back, except that I'm not sure about the tides, and I'm scared to risk going back into that tunnel.'

'*Tunnel*?' I repeated.

'It leads from the cave. I watched the fishermen with the boat. They go out to pull up a lobster pot, and bring the lobsters back in the boat. The boat disappeared, but soon the two men came out on to the sand and went off home up the cliff. So I climbed down, and found the mouth of the cave – and there was the boat moored inside it.

'I had my pencil torch with me, and it's dark in the cave, so I shone the torch around, and found the opening to the tunnel. The tunnel is amazing! I climbed in. You can walk along it standing upright – at least you could, if it wasn't slippery and rough underfoot. I wanted to see where it led to, but it goes on and on, and then I slipped, and dropped the torch, and it went out.

'It was pitch dark, and I was scrabbling about trying to find the torch when the strap of the case of the field glasses slid off my shoulder. They're not *lost*. I mean they're there, on the floor of the tunnel.' I stared at him aghast. 'Then you'll have to go back and get them! Why did you leave them there?'

'I couldn't find them, Lorna! It was pitch black, and I was on my knees feeling around for them and the torch for *ages*. I could hear the sea, like waves crashing in, and the tide had been coming in when I went into the cave. I thought the sea might come in and fill the tunnel and I'd never get out. I could only see a sort of dim patch of light far away at the entrance to the tunnel, so I scrambled back to the entrance, and there was about a foot of water in the cave by then. I got my trainers soaked, going through it.'

'So,' I said, 'we've got to take a torch and go back for the field glasses, and just hope they haven't been submerged in water, and didn't break when you dropped them.'

'Not *you*,' he said. 'I'll go by myself. But when? The tides are different every day. I've got to find out from someone local if the tide fills up that tunnel when it comes in, and if it does, when is the safest time to go, so I don't get drowned.'

'I think you'd better own up to Dad,' I said. 'He'll be more angry about you taking that risk – going in there on your own, than he will about the field glasses.'

'Lorna, I *can't*!' He looked away from me and muttered, 'I'm not afraid of him being mad at me. It's just that he'll never trust me again, will he?'

'He will. He'll think you've learned your lesson.'

'No,' William said. 'I'll get the field glasses back. You'd think Andrew would know all about tides, but all he seems to know is that low tide is about six hours after high tide! Not that I've told him what I've done. If he knew there was a cave there'd be no peace till he'd been in it.'

'That's true,' I agreed. 'Those fishermen, with the boat – they'd know, wouldn't they? Why not hang around till they come again?'

It was all we could think of. 'But don't go in there alone again,' I warned him. 'Listen carefully to what they say about the tides, and ask if the water goes into the tunnel. I'll come with you to find the field glasses. I could stay in the cave and yell to you if the water starts coming in fast.'

'Oh, thanks, Lorn,' he sighed. 'And you won't tell Mum or Dad?'

I glared at him. 'Have I ever sneaked on you?' I demanded.

He shook his head, grinned, and said goodnight.

Before I put my light out, I took Mike's photograph from the bedside table. As I gazed at it, he seemed to smile at me in the old, intimate way, as if we shared a secret. I felt my throat tighten with tears. He'd said I was possessive . . . Not like Zara who didn't make demands . . . What demands had I made? All I'd done was want to be with him, even to the point of considering leaving home, and living in that bed-sitter!

I slid out of bed and took the photograph, and the other one of Mike and me standing beside his car, and put them into my dressing table drawer. After a moment, I put the china cat in there, too, and the coral necklace.

Now there was only the bedside lamp beside me on the table as I lay down to sleep. Before putting the light out, I gazed around the big airy room at white walls and dark furniture, the soft pink carpet and matching silky curtains.

Tomorrow, I'd unpack my boxes and put up my posters.

Chapter 6

Next day, when I told Mum I was going out with Gwillym, I saw the relief in her eyes, and felt a flash of irritation, until I remembered what Dad had said about her never showing her reluctance to come here. I realized she was just anxious for me to make friends locally.

I helped with the housework, and we sat down for coffee at about eleven o'clock. I took a breath and said, 'Mum – I'm sorry about the way I've behaved since we came here.'

She just smiled and said 'I'm sure you couldn't help it.'

'But – you didn't want to come here, either, yet you pretended to like it, didn't you?'

'We had no choice,' she said. 'So I looked at the advantages, and found there were quite a few.'

'Such as?' I asked.

'Well, your father doesn't have to commute to the City every day. The three of you will go to very good schools, and the boys love the freedom of the country and seaside.'

'But that's *us*,' I said. 'What about *you*?'

'If you're all happy, then I'm happy,' she answered.

I blinked. 'But,' I persisted, 'The Barbican, the Festival Hall, the Opera – and you used to love the West End shops. Then there were all your committees.'

She laughed. 'I'm glad not to be on any committees at last! But, yes, I shall miss the concerts, and the art galleries. But we've come to a land of music. And I love the house! It has real character.'

'So that's how you do it,' I said. 'You just add up the advantages and concentrate on those.'

'Yes, I suppose I do,' she answered. 'But – what about you? Something happened this weekend. If you'd rather not tell me, of course . . . '

There was only Mum and me in the house. Suddenly, I longed to tell her everything, but how could I? How could I hurt her by telling her I'd planned to leave home and get a job and live in London?

I told her about Mike only writing to me once, when I'd written to him lots of times, and about his never being at home when I phoned, and never once phoning me. 'But I just kept on hoping,' I admitted. 'I thought, when I saw him again, I'd be able to get him back.'

I missed out everything about the bed-sitter, and got to the part where I discovered Mike had been seeing Zara again, and she interrupted with, 'But you were already feeling differently about him, weren't you, before you discovered that. You were annoyed when he arrived late at the party and talked about the car all the time.'

'Well, Mum, he was *boring* everyone!' I said. 'It was a *party*! People were being polite, pretending to listen, and he didn't realize it!'

He lips twitched slightly, at the edge of a smile, but she went on, 'You never found him boring before though, and he always did – er – go on a lot about cars.'

'I suppose he did,' I agreed. 'I never noticed it before.'

'Perhaps you were seeing him afresh,' she suggested, 'having been parted for so long.'

I thought about that for a moment. Was it possible? I'd never been angry or irritated with Mike before.

Mum said, 'So – you decided to part with Mike?'

I nodded, deciding that I didn't have to explain that it wasn't quite like that.

'We had an argument,' I said. 'He said I was possessive. Do you think I was?'

'If you were, it didn't bother him when you were together most of the time,' she replied. 'He didn't complain about it then, did he?'

'Never,' I answered. 'And I've learned something, Mum. I'll never get involved with a boy like that again – *never*.'

'Perhaps you didn't really know Mike well enough,' she said quietly. 'It takes a long time to get to know someone really well.'

'And in the end it usually isn't worth it,' I muttered. 'From now on, I'm not going to bother with boyfriends at all.'

I felt much happier, more relaxed, now that Mum knew the situation. She said, 'I'll have to call Andrew in. I must take him to the village to get his hair cut.'

'I'll take him,' I offered.

'Will you really? It would save time. Once I get a car, it'll be a lot easier for us all, but there hasn't been time to look around for one yet.'

As Andrew and I walked up the hill, he was complaining bitterly about having to go to a Ladies' Hairdresser's. 'They do men as well,' I told him. 'There isn't a men's hairdresser's here. Once Mum gets a car I expect she'll take you into Gwenally.'

He glowered and began kicking a stone along the pavement. 'I don't want my hair cut by a *girl*!' he muttered. 'When Mum took me in to make the appointment, everything smelled of women's perfume and stuff! Anyway, why can't I come up here on my own?'

'Because you might come home with a Mohican,' I replied.

Luckily, there was an older boy having his hair cut when we got to the hairdresser's, and Andrew was shown to the chair next to him. 'I'll leave you here,' I said, 'and come back in about ten minutes. I've got to get some bread. O.K.?'

He jerked his head in a nod, and I left him sitting there, his lower lip stuck out, his eyes narrowed.

In the baker's I ran straight into Gwillym, who offered me a lift home. 'Thanks,' I said, 'but I've got to wait for Andrew. He's having his hair cut.'

'Well, that won't take long,' he said. 'I can wait. Let's have a coffee.'

We went into the Tea Shop next to the baker's. 'He'll be furious if I'm late,' I said. 'He's already annoyed at having to go to a Ladies' hairdresser.'

Gwillym laughed, and we sat at a table by the window. We were talking of nothing in particular when I remembered William's problem, and realized that Gwillym might know about the tides.

When I told him what had happened, he said, 'Yes, I know the cave, and I used to explore the tunnel with other boys when I was a kid. It's quite safe and never gets water in the tunnel. I'll go in this afternoon, when the cave is dry and get the field glasses.'

'But I can't put you to all that trouble,' I gasped. 'If the tide doesn't flood the tunnel, I can go in myself.'

'We'll both go,' he suggested. 'Meet me on the beach, about two o'clock? Wear old clothes, and bring a torch.'

I warned him to say nothing to Andrew or my parents as we crossed the road to the hairdresser's.

Andrew didn't notice me at the reception desk. He was too busy talking to the hairdresser as she dusted hairs off his cape, and then showed him the mirror. He gazed into it, nodded, and went on, 'Come to our house any time, and I'll let you look through it. It's absolutely *brill*!'

He was talking about his telescope! 'You're a very lucky young man,' she said seriously as she removed the cape, 'to have a valuable thing like that. And when you get into the Navy, you'll be one step ahead of the others, won't you, what with all you'll have learnt, watching ships and that?'

On the way home, Andrew said, 'It wasn't like I thought. I told her I didn't want any of the perfume on my hair, and she said she quite understood, and never used it for gentlemen, anyway. Lots of men go there, Lorna. Grown ups as well as boys. It's *Unisex*, she told me.'

When we got home, William had had an early lunch and gone off to Jones's farm having offered to help unload a delivery of cattle feed, so I couldn't put him out of his misery about the tunnel. It meant that

Gwillym and I would be alone this afternoon, as I knew William would have insisted on coming too.

Gwillym was already on the beach when I arrived, in my oldest jeans, and carrying a sweater as he'd said it would be cold in the tunnel.

'If the tunnel did get flooded,' he smiled, 'it wouldn't have been much use. It was cut out of the rock by smugglers and it used to lead to Peter's cellar where the goods were stored.'

I looked back along the shore to where Peter's cottage stood. 'It goes all that way?' I gasped.

'Not now. It's been blocked off for donkey's years. There are lots of tunnels like it, all around the coast. Every seaport or coastal village in Wales has its stock of smuggler's tales, but our bit of coastline has a history of pirates and wreckers, as well as smugglers.'

'I saw a sailing ship that looked like a pirate ship,' I told him. 'It was the day I found Jack on the beach. Andrew's seen it too, through his telescope. I suppose it's a training ship. Is there a naval training school near here?'

He frowned. 'Not that I know of. What did the ship look like?'

We were walking along the sand towards the end of the reef, and I said, 'It looked beautiful. It had two masts. Andrew said it was a brig – if you know what that means. It looked like something out of an old painting, and it moved so smoothly. Then it appeared to go into the side of the cliff and disappear. I suppose it went into the next cove, out of my view, but I couldn't work out how.'

'That's amazing,' Gwillym said quietly. 'I – I just can't believe it!'

I glanced at him, puzzled. 'Why not? There could be one of those summer courses in sailing around here somewhere.'

He hesitated, then said, 'Yes. Yes, I expect you're right. It's just that – well, there's a legend about a pirate ship. The facts are that the Price's house was owned by a pirate. He and his three sons became very rich, robbing merchant ships in these waters. They also robbed smugglers who'd been to France to buy their cargo and were bringing it here to avoid paying duty . . . What made you think the ship you saw was like a pirate ship? I mean – it wasn't flying the skull and crossbones, was it?'

I laughed. 'No! I can't think why I thought it looked like a pirate ship really. It was black, perhaps that's why. Or perhaps it reminded me of a pirate ship I've seen in a film at some time. Tell me the legend.'

'Oh – it's probably a load of rubbish,' he smiled. 'Let's get those field glasses first. Here's the cave.'

We stepped out of blazing sunlight into deep gloom. The floor of the cave was soft with clean sand washed in by the sea, and I blinked, trying to make out the entrance to the tunnel.

'Over here,' Gwillym called, and played his torch on the wall of the cave to reveal a wide opening about two feet above ground level. 'I'll go first,' he said. 'Oh – this takes me back to my carefree boyhood! Be careful, and shine your torch, too, because the ground isn't that level.'

The chill hit me as we made our way slowly, and I was glad of my thick sweater.

'I wonder how far in he went?' Gwillym said. 'This tunnel goes on for about half a mile.'

I shuddered. Already I felt uncomfortable. Our torches showed only black rock all around us, the ceiling uneven, so that in places we had to crouch. Our voices sounded strange – sort of metallic and hollow, and made a faint echo which lingered in my ears. I would be very glad to get out of here, back into fresh air and daylight!

'What's that sighing sound?' I asked nervously.

'The sea,' Gwillym answered. 'He did say he *dropped* the field glasses case, didn't he? I did wonder if it might be caught by the strap on a rock projection. I don't want to miss it.'

'He said he dropped it,' I answered, hating the way the sound of my voice whipped back at me, and seemed to wrap itself around my head, still echoing in my ears. 'Isn't it *cold* in here?'

'Yes. Never gets any sunlight,' he replied.

We didn't talk again for some time. We must by now have been in the tunnel for ten minutes. I realized how frightening it must have been for William when he dropped his torch. To be deep inside the cliff, like this, in pitch darkness, wondering if the tide might rush in . . .

'Surely he wouldn't go any further than this,' I murmured, and the sound came back, muffled, yet changed, so that it seemed as if my voice was booming.

'Well, I don't think we can have missed the case,'

Gwillym said. 'If I missed it, you'd see it, wouldn't you?'

'Yes,' I agreed. I wanted nothing more than to find the field glasses and get out of here. I was staring at every inch of ground I walked over, hoping desperately to see a brown leather case, sweeping my torch from side to side before going on, yet afraid of getting too far behind Gwillym.

The tunnel was wider now, and in the torch light I saw Gwillym turn and smile at me. 'You all right back there?' he asked.

'Well – it's not exactly my idea of fun,' I answered.

'The going gets easier now,' he said, waiting until I was beside him. He took my hand. 'The ground is a bit rougher now,' he added, 'Be careful not to slip, but at least we can stand upright from now on.'

His hand was warm as it gripped mine firmly. Suddenly, I felt safe. We floundered on, skidding over smooth rock, stumbling against projections, going slowly, scanning the ground.

'This would be where he fell over,' Gwillym said. 'We'll find it any minute now.'

And he was right. I've never felt such wonderful relief as when we both exclaimed, '*There*!' and shone our torches to beam in on the leather case, lying to the side of the tunnel under a small outcrop of the rock.

Gwillym picked it up and slung it over his shoulder. 'There's the torch,' he said, bending to pick it up. A pencil torch isn't much good to explore caves with!'

'He just happened to have it with him,' I said.

We turned and began to go back. Gwillym took my

hand again, and all my fear left me. I could see the dim patch of light ahead now. When we reached the narrow part, Gwillym went in front again, and I missed the warmth of his hand holding mine, but I wasn't afraid now, so long as I was close to him.

It was good to be back in the sunshine, stripping off our sweaters on the beach and sitting down on the sand with our backs to the reef.

'Thanks very much, Gwillym,' I said. 'William will be very grateful, and so am I!'

Gwillym laughed. 'But I quite enjoyed it! I don't often get to be with pretty girls in dark tunnels.'

I giggled. 'You mean your girlfriends actually *refuse* to crawl along in cold damp caverns with you?'

'They have no sense of adventure,' he grinned.

'You were going to tell me the legend,' I reminded him, 'about the pirate ship.'

'Oh – there are so many legends about this coast,' he replied, evasively.

'But you said there actually *was* a pirate who lived here,' I prompted him. 'You said he lived in the house where the Price's live now.'

He nodded. 'Henry Standing built that house. He was both a smuggler and a pirate. He had a big ship and a crew of over seventy men. In the eighteenth century, he was regarded as a sort of Robin Hood, and treated as the local squire.

'His ship was coming home, laden with goods, on a calm sea, when it suddenly went down. People watching, waiting with rowing boats to go out and bring in his cargo, couldn't believe what they'd seen. The ship just disappeared.'

'They must have struck a rock,' I said.

'No. Only a few of the crew survived, and none of them had any explanation for what happened. But then, perhaps in those days it wasn't all that unusual. It's a recorded fact that in January 1868, in a single night, nineteen ships were wrecked off the coast not far from here. The graves of the dead sailors are in Llanmadoc churchyard. There was no storm, just a heavy swell of the tide which was on flood.'

'But — what's the legend about the pirate ship?' I asked. It seemed as if he didn't want to tell me.

'Oh — some people claim to have seen its ghost, that's all,' he smiled.

'Well — I don't think Andrew would be likely to see a ghost-ship,' I smiled, 'and he logged it in his book. The ship I saw didn't look at all ghostly, either.'

'You said it seemed to go into the side of the cliff,' he murmured. 'That's how Standing's ship appeared to the watchers on the shore. In fact, it sunk. The wreck is down there still.'

I shivered despite the blazing sun. 'And what is supposed to happen,' I asked, 'to people who see the ghost ship?'

He smiled. 'I expect they just get the fright of their lives, if they know about the ship,' he said. 'If they don't, they assume there's a training depot somewhere near.'

'And', I thought, 'that's all you're going to tell me, so seeing the ghost ship is probably some sort of omen — a sign of death or something equally ghastly!'

'I'll stick to my theory about a training ship,' I said. 'Surely ghost ships don't appear in *telescopes*!'

Gwillym glanced at his watch. 'I've promised to help Dad with surgery this afternoon,' he said, 'so I'll have to start back now.'

We walked back along the beach, and I wished he'd take my hand as he had in the tunnel. Silly, really, because I wasn't in the least interested in Gwillym, except as a friend.

'What do people wear for the folk club?' I asked.

He looked at me, surprised. '*Wear*?'

'I mean, do they dress up, like for a disco? I haven't been to a folk club for ages – the one we had at home packed up, but I do remember everyone just wore jeans and sweaters.'

'Oh, I see,' he nodded. 'Just jeans. It's all very informal. I'll call for you around seven thirty if that's OK?'

'Fine,' I agreed.

In the afternoon, I put up some of my posters and arranged my collection of wooden animals on the shelves in my bedroom. I'd examined the field glasses carefully, and there was no damage at all. The leather case wasn't even scuffed. I'd put it in the attic where Andrew's telescope was, as if it had never been removed from there, and wished William would come home so I could take the worry off his mind.

And, while I was in the attic, I'd looked at Andrew's logbook again, checking for his sighting of the pirate ship. There was just the one entry, four days before the day on which I'd seen it just before I found Jack.

I turned the pages. He *had* been watching on the day I'd seen the ship, until seven o'clock, when he'd written, 'End of Watch', signed his name, 'Andrew James Collins' and ruled it off. A few moments later, he'd have seen me appear over the cliff edge and race along towards the vet's house.

I scanned the notes he'd made. There was no mention of the sailing ship he'd called a brig, and I didn't see how he could have missed it.

He'd recorded that Mr Morgan took his dog, Bess, for a walk in the adjacent cove at 18.35 hrs. '18.40 hrs. Mrs Thomas took in washing. 2 pink nightdresses, 4 pairs ladys pantys, 1 brazier.' He hadn't seen me, sitting on the beach. I'd have been hidden by the cliff.

But *why* hadn't he seen the sailing ship? Could I actually have seen a ghost ship? I dismissed the idea nervously. It would have been floating in the air, about a foot above the water, or something, wouldn't it? The sails were slack, and it moved smoothly, at a reasonable speed . . . *The sails were slack*? But there had been a strong wind that day! Mr Evans had insisted I put on the jacket!

I was ready when Gwillym called for me, and we drove up through the village to Gwenally, and parked on a paved area outside a modern red brick building called the Community Hall.

Inside, it was quite small, but there was a proper stage and comfortable seating. People went on arriving until the place was packed, and people were standing at the back.

The main group was called The Shepherds – three brothers, who wore shepherds' smocks, and they started off with 'Whisky in the Jar', which I hadn't heard for ages. They had lovely voices and played accordion, guitar, fiddle, and flute in turn – really good musicians. They went on to 'Wild Rover', then a song of their own composition, which we could join in with, in the chorus.

There were one or two solo singers as guest artistes, then the interval when we had coffee in a room at the side of the building, and Gwillym asked if I was enjoying it. 'It's great,' I nodded, and I meant it. There was such a friendly atmosphere, and people kept coming to talk to Gwillym and he introduced them to me. There were two girls who said they'd be in the sixth forms at the Grammar school next term, and we promised to look out for each other next Monday.

One of the girls, Nerys Griffiths, said, 'We get lots of privileges in the sixth forms. We have our own common room, and we don't have to wear school uniform, and games aren't compulsory. You'll like it, once you get to know people.'

It was in the second half that I got the shock of my life. The Shepherds did two more songs, then asked if anyone from the audience would come up on the stage and sing.

No one moved, but people were turning round to look at someone I thought must be sitting near us, saying, 'Come on then!' and, 'Be a sport – come on!'. It was all good-humoured. I looked around curiously, to see who it was that they wanted to sing. Then the man on the stage said, 'What's the matter, Gwillym? Got laryngitis?'

I think my mouth must have fallen open in surprise.

'I won't go if you'd rather I didn't,' he muttered. 'I haven't brought my guitar anyway, so—'

'Of course I don't mind!' I gasped. They'd started chanting now, but in a nice, friendly way, 'Gwillym Evans. Gwillym Evans!'

Everyone started clapping as he got up and went to the stage and leapt up. One of The Shepherds adjusted the microphone, the other stood beside Gwillym with his guitar, obviously ready to accompany him. They spoke together, then turned to the audience, who were clamouring for something in Welsh which I didn't understand. It was like being in a foreign country, and just for a moment, I felt shut out. I couldn't even catch the words they were calling, except the last two which sounded like 'Gwynneth Gwyn.'

Nerys Griffiths who was sitting behind me, leaned over and said, 'It's about the ripening of the corn. I don't think there are any English words to it. They always want him to sing this.'

As soon as Gwillym started to sing, I recognized the tune, though I couldn't think where I'd heard it before. It was beautiful! He had a strong tenor voice, and I felt a warm glow spread right through me. When he reached the high notes, my throat felt tight and tears pricked at my eyes. I just couldn't believe it was Gwillym up there, with that wonderful voice, so relaxed, and with all the meaning of the song in the expressions on his face.

The moment he finished, there was complete silence in the hall, as if no one had been breathing, and then the applause broke out, and as he began to come down off the stage, they stamped and yelled, 'Encore!', and one of The Shepherds dragged him back.

This time, he sang 'Bridge Over Troubled Water' which I knew, because Dad had the record, and I'd always liked it, and again, the emotion he put into it brought tears to my eyes.

When at last they let him go and he came back to his seat, I grabbed his arm and said, 'It was *beautiful* - wonderful! I didn't even know you could sing!'

He smiled and took my hand, and held it, and I felt the same strange feeling I'd felt in the tunnel. A man with a long black beard went up and sang something in Welsh in a good baritone voice, and when the applause started, I had to take my hand from Gwillym's to join in, though I'd rather not have clapped, however rude it seemed. But, as the next singer went up on stage, Gwillym reached for my hand again, and I felt his fingers curl round mine, then our hands were locked together, gently, but firmly.

On the drive home, I was warm with excitement until I remembered something! It was when I'd seen Mike on stage as Hamlet in the school play that I'd first felt attracted to him. I had a vivid flash of memory seeing him, centre stage, delivering those marvellous lines, looking wonderful, saying, 'Whether 'tis nobler in the mind to suffer the slings and arrows . . . '

Well, *that* wasn't going to happen again – not to me!

'Did you really enjoy it?' Gwillym asked anxiously.

I laughed. 'Wasn't it obvious? My hands are still stinging with clapping so much!' And, I thought, the hand you held feels cold now, and I wish you could drive with one hand, so I could feel close to you again, but that's something I'm going to get over, very quickly.

'I honestly didn't intend to go on stage tonight,' Gwillym said quietly. 'I hope you didn't think I was showing off.'

'You weren't,' I said. 'They insisted, and I don't blame them. Have you had singing lessons? I mean, you sounded professional.'

'I've had the training most Welsh boys have,' he replied. 'It's usual, if you have a decent treble voice, to join a choir at about eight years old. The training is very good.'

We left the lights of Gwenally, and turned on to the unlit coast road, where the car's headlights scythed the total darkness. In the dimness of the car I felt Gwillym's presence powerfully, as I watched his strong capable hands on the steering wheel. I felt close to him, as if I'd known him all my life, instead of for just a few hours.

'Thank you for a lovely evening, Gwillym,' I said quietly.

He gave me a quick, quizzical glance. 'Thank you for coming with me,' he replied. 'You're great company, Lorna. I was wondering if you'd like to come out with me again — one afternoon this week perhaps.'

'I'd like that,' I nodded.

'Tomorrow?' he asked.

'Great!'

'We'll go to the Gower. There are lots of lovely, quiet beaches on the Gower, and it seems as if the weather's changed, so bring your swimming things. I'll call for you at around two o'clock.'

Before I went up to bed that night, I looked in the bookcase for something I remembered that Mrs Morgan, the newsagent, had given to William. It had been in a box full of books and pamphlets she'd had left over from the holiday season – a thick paperback book with a black cover, entitled, 'Myths and Legends of Wales' – or something similar to that.

As I put the book on my bedside table, I noticed the record I'd played over and over for the past few weeks – 'Flip Side of Loving'. I put it in a drawer, thinking about the words of the lyric, 'The flip side of loving is hating.'

I didn't hate Mike. What I felt was more like bitter disappointment. Maybe that was the meaning of the lyric. You have to feel strongly about someone to love him or to hate him, but, if it all fades away into disappointment and hurt, there's just nothing left.

I climbed into bed and opened the book. Gwillym hadn't been exaggerating when he'd said there were hundreds of legends about this area. Eventually, I found what I was looking for: 'The Haunting of Caeraddon Bay'.

Henry Standing had a chapter all to himself, which I read, fascinated. He was a complex character, on the one hand a pirate, who would seize a cargo and sometimes take the ship as well, and a smuggler with a well-organised racket in which he employed his three sons. On the other hand, he really cared about people, and the villagers regarded him as their squire, to whom they owed loyalty, and gratitude.

'No one in Caeraddon was afraid to ask Henry Standing for help, and it was never refused . . . '

The chapter ended with the sudden, inexplicable sinking of the pirate ship Dark Lady, and the grief of the villagers at the death of Henry Standing. They had no faith that his eldest son would carry on in his father's caring role for them.

'There are numerous records of sightings of Henry Standing's ship, even in recent months. The ghost ship is seen at the exact spot where it sunk on the tenth of October 1522 – the tenth day of the tenth month of a year in which the digits add up to ten, at ten o'clock in the morning! The figure ten crops up again in the report that, of a crew of seventy five men, only ten survived.

'It is generally believed that the sighting of the ghost ship may be Henry Standing's way of continuing to protect the people of Caeraddon, by warning them of impending danger, as they had always warned him of traps set by the Excise men. So, if you see the ghost ship, take care not to indulge in dangerous activities during the ensuing ten days!

'There is a widely held belief that the warning concerns affairs of the heart as well as physical dangers, since Henry Standing suffered himself at the hands of a scheming and unfaithful wife, therefore no hasty decisions in these matters should be taken for at least ten days after a sighting of the ghost ship. Marriages have been known to be postponed in Caeraddon, because one of the prospective partners has seen the Dark Lady, though it could be suggested that this might be a convenient excuse for anyone having second thoughts!'

Although the story was written tongue-in-cheek, I counted on my fingers the number of days since I'd seen the ghost ship. Six! I had four more days in which to watch my step. Or had Henry Standing meant to warn me not to leave home for Mike?

I closed the book and put it on the bedside table. The ship I'd seen wasn't a vision swathed in mist, as ghost ships must be. And it had gone out of sight, not 'disappeared'.

But now I knew why Gwillym hadn't told me the full story. Anyone believing that legend might be too scared to get out of bed for ten days after seeing the Dark Lady!

Chapter 7

I knew, as soon as I awoke next morning, that there was something different about the day. I opened my curtains and saw what it was. Already the sun was high in a clear blue sky. The sea looked like a sheet of still water, inky blue, glittering in the sunlight, as if millions of silver coins were scattered on its surface.

It was going to be a glorious day, and I was going out with Gwillym.

After breakfast, I went to see Peter, to ask about Jack, and to tell him I'd seen the television programme about him. Jack limped out to greet me, one hind leg in plaster, but I could see he was recovering well.

Peter insisted in breaking off work, saying he was dying for coffee, so I made it, on the little stove he had in the studio, while he washed clay off his hands at the sink.

'So you came back,' he said. 'Did you change your mind?'

As we had coffee, I told him the whole story, not the edited version I'd given to Mum. When I finished I could see relief in his eyes.

'I'm sorry you had to go through all that, Lorna,' he said, 'but you seem to be coping very well.'

'I suppose I am,' I said, surprised to realize it. 'Still, I've not had much time to think since I got home. I went out with Gwillym last night.'

I glanced up at Megan's portrait on the shelf. It still wasn't finished. 'You said my problems could be solved, but yours couldn't,' I said. 'But if it's money — because Megan has so much — well, you may become rich and famous one day, Peter, and have more money than she has.'

He half smiled. 'But I don't care about fame and fortune, Lorna. I just want to do the work I'm so lucky to be doing. Megan's more likely to become famous than I am.'

I looked at him in surprise. 'Oh? How?'

'She's an actress.'

'Really? No one told me that! I might have seen her on television.'

'She's not done much television work. She was in a play in the West End last year though. Most of her work is in films. She's in that film they're making near here, in Pentreath Bay on the Gower.'

'They're making a film, near here?'

'Yes – well, they're doing the location work here, because it's a period film about smuggling and they're using some old sailing ships. This location is ideal, with no modern buildings to intrude on the landscape.'

So there was the explanation of my ghost ship! I didn't know whether to be relieved or disappointed.

'Megan's portrait won't be finished,' he said, noticing that I was looking at it. 'She and I have split up. She's going to marry the American film producer, Andy Miller.'

I stared at him, horrified. 'Oh, *Peter*! And you let me ramble on about my silly affairs!'

'There's nothing silly about you and Mike,' he answered.

'But – you and Megan were old enough to get *married*!'

'Old enough – yes. But in reality, how could I expect Megan to come and live here, with me? They're selling the house. Her father is going to live in Jersey as a tax exile, and when the film's finished, Megan is flying to California.'

I didn't know what to say. I felt hot with shame that I'd bothered him with my problems.

'Megan wanted me to be famous,' he said, half smiling. 'She wanted me to let her support me, while I did my own work instead of taking commissions, and she had connections in New York, where she wanted to plan a major exhibition for me. I could never have agreed to that. If I get anywhere, it has to be by my own efforts.'

I nodded. 'Yes. But perhaps she couldn't understand that. I think lots of people want to be famous, and they don't care about how.'

'That wasn't the reason for the break,' he said. 'It was much simpler than that. She met Andy Miller and fell in love with him. He's much more suitable for her than I would have been. Megan is ambitious and she wants to work in American films.'

I sighed. 'I wish there was something I could do to help.'

'And you know, Lorna,' he said, 'more than most people, that nothing helps. You said you were living in a dream, with Mike. I think Megan was in love with a dream – not with me. She was in love with what she thought I could become, not with the raw material that was me. Do you know what I mean?'

'Yes, I do,' I answered. 'I expect you can't concentrate on anything. It's awful. I know how it is.'

'I can lose myself in my work,' he said.

'With me,' I murmured, 'it was Mum and Dad and the boys. Coming home, and finding I was, sort of, needed.'

'We're both lucky, really,' he smiled.

As I walked slowly home, I couldn't stop thinking about Peter, and I was really glad I'd learned my lesson never to get involved with a boy again. I could practise my new resolution on Gwillym. He just wanted someone to share the last bit of the holidays with, and that was what I wanted, too.

He called for me at two o'clock and we drove out on to the coast road. 'Shall we find a beach and swim for a bit?' he asked. 'Then we could have tea somewhere.'

'Great!' I nodded. It was really hot now, and in my yellow cotton dress with the brown belt that matched my shoulder bag and sandals, I thought I looked good as well as feeling comfortable. Gwillym was wearing oatmeal coloured trousers and a black shirt. He looked fantastic!

He began listing the choice of beaches, finishing with, 'Bracelet Bay, Limeslade Bay, and from Caswell Bay there's a path that leads to Brandy Cove – you can guess how it got its name!'

I laughed. 'Didn't anyone ever do any honest work around here in the olden days?' I asked.

'There wasn't much honest work to be had,' he smiled. 'Oddly enough, it was the rich landowners who financed the smuggling. I think they regarded smuggling as honest work.'

'*What*?'

'Well, they bought the goods, legally, in France. They just avoided paying duty on them. They were tax-evaders, not thieves.'

'I see,' I nodded, 'and the pirates were really doing the merchant ships a big favour by stealing their cargoes?'

He laughed. 'Off-hand, I can't think of a good excuse for the pirates.'

He parked the car and we went down to a tiny cove

backed by thick woodland, where the sand was soft and warm, and there was no one else on the beach.

'Even in the holiday season,' Gwillym said, 'there are always quiet places like this, if you look for them.'

The water was warm, and we swam together, keeping fairly close in to shore. It was sheer bliss. I could have gone on swimming for ages when Gwillym turned and made for the beach, so I followed him. We spread out our towels and lay in the sun.

I told him about the book I'd read in bed last night, about myths and legends. 'But I have an explanation for my pirate ship,' I said. 'Peter told me there's a film being made near here, using sailing ships.'

'Did you read about the saint who lived in the woods back there, hundreds of years ago?' he asked.

'No. Tell me about him.'

'Not "him" – it was a girl,' he said. 'A young prince was out hunting one day, and he chased a hare into a thicket. He parted the undergrowth, and found the saint, with the frightened hare sitting on her lap. He was so amazed that he gave her the woodland, and the right of sanctuary for ever.

'Later, several women joined the saint and she founded a convent. She's buried in the little church you can see through the trees, and she still watches over the woods, so that no harm ever comes to anyone walking there.'

I smiled. 'It's a nice story,' I said, 'but it wouldn't be much use telling my father I was going walking alone in those woods at night because a saint was still watching over them.'

I sat up and looked down at him. 'You don't believe in that sort of thing, do you?' I asked.

'Why not?' he grinned. 'I'll bet nothing like that ever happened in Wimbledon.'

I laughed, and he reached up suddenly, and pulled me down, and kissed me. It was a gentle kiss, but it seemed to go on and on. When we parted, I stared at him, surprised. I'd never been kissed like that before.

We swam again, dried off in the sun, then wandered up through the woods, along a steeply rising path which led to a tiny village clustered around the church where the saint was buried.

'There's a café at the end of the street,' Gwillym said. 'I'm dying of thirst, aren't you?'

In the café, we sat beside a window which overlooked the bay, and the waitress brought tall glasses of pineapple juice and a plate of fresh baked scones.

The middle-aged couple at a nearby table were talking to each other in Welsh, and again I had the feeling of being in a foreign country, yet today, I felt as if I belonged here.

I'd heard Gwillym and his father exchange the odd remark in Welsh, on the day we found Jack on the beach. Now I realized that when they were alone, they'd speak Welsh all the time.

After tea, we drove to an inland village and watched a potter working, making jugs and bowls which would later be fired and glazed, like the ones for sale which were on the shelves. They were in lovely shades of green and brown and blue. While Gwillym was asking the potter about glazes, I bought a jug for Mum. It was so pretty, coloured with many different shades of green which all blended together.

It was past seven o'clock, and becoming noticeably cooler. Gwillym suggested we should drive back to Swansea and have a pizza.

There were lots of people around our own age in the café, some of them obviously dressed for going on to a disco. We ordered our pizzas and Gwillym said, 'We could go to a disco if you like, or the cinema, or have a look around the town.'

I didn't want to go to a disco. I wanted just to be with him, to go on finding out more about him. I'd never talked so much, or asked so many questions.

'You decide,' I said. 'I haven't seen the town, and I'm quite happy just walking around.'

We lingered over coffee, still finding so much to talk about. 'Looks as if a storm's coming up,' Gwillym murmured, glancing out of the window. The sky was dark now, with thick black clouds.

We wandered around Swansea, looking at the shops, then went into the park, and, as it was really dark by now, we went back to the car to shelter from the storm that threatened.

As we drove into Caeraddon village, Gwillym said, 'I think I must have bored you stiff, Lorna. I haven't talked so much for ages.'

'Oh *no*!' I gasped. '*I've* talked so much that I was wondering if you still thought I was good company!'

He took his hand from the steering wheel and laid it briefly on my arm. 'The best,' he smiled.

As he stopped the car at our gate, I saw that the front

door was open. Mum came out and ran towards the car, and I knew something was wrong. Fear gripped me as I saw her face, white and anxious, and I leapt out of the car.

'What's happened?' I cried, trembling suddenly.

'The boys,' she gasped. 'They're missing. They went out after dinner, about seven o'clock, and haven't come back. We've phoned everyone we can think of. Lorna – can you think where they might have gone?'

We followed her into the living room. Dad was out with the car, driving around, searching. 'I daren't leave the house, in case they come back, or there's news of them,' Mum said. 'Something must have happened. William would have brought Andrew back by eight o'clock otherwise.'

A cold chill spread through me. 'Where did they say they were going?' I asked.

'They didn't. We thought they were in the orchard. Lorna, it's past eleven o'clock! Dad phoned the police at nine. They told him to ring back later if the boys didn't turn up – it was too early to think of them as missing, and boys often did this sort of thing – but William and Andrew wouldn't, would they, Lorna? I *know* something's happened to them, and I don't know what to do!'

Gwillym said, 'You've phoned all their friends?'

Mum nodded. 'Everyone's offered to go out and look for them. People are so kind! Mr Jones at the farm has looked in all his outbuildings, in case they'd been accidentally locked in. Peter Jackson is out with Jack, looking all along the beaches.' Her voice dropped as she whispered, 'Dad phoned the coastguard, and they said they'd send out a patrol, but it's getting so dark now . . . Oh, Gwillym, can *you* think what might have happened? Did you ever do anything like this when you were a boy?'

'I expect I did,' Gwillym murmured. 'You know what boys are! What I think is – they'll have gone somewhere and lost their way back. It's so dark tonight, because of the clouds. It's very easy to lose your way when it gets dark suddenly, like it did tonight. And they are together. William is twelve and very sensible.'

I knew he was trying to think of something to comfort Mum, and I saw relief dawn in her eyes briefly, but I still felt a cold sense of dread – and of all the stupid things to think about – I remembered that Andrew had seen the pirate ship too! The warning of danger!

'We'd better not waste time,' I said. 'Where's the big torch? Gwillym and I can go in different directions—'

'No,' he said. 'You could lose your way, too. We'll go together. I've got my boots in the car. You get yours on while I get my torch from the glove-box.'

I pulled on my boots and anorak and grabbed a torch, and gave Mum a quick hug. 'We'll look *everywhere*,' I promised, 'and we'll keep checking back to see if they've turned up.'

I imagined awful things as Gwillym and I set off. I thought of the boys lying with broken limbs at the foot of the cliff, or cut off by the tide. I'd never known before how dark it is without street lighting.

'We'll start with the farm,' Gwillym said. 'They were always around there when I was working for Mr Jones. They could have started back through the woodland and lost their way. But can you think of anything they've said lately, about anywhere else? Anything new they're interested in?'

My mind refused to work. I was numb with fear, yet I knew I had to think hard, to try to remember any small thing that might give a clue.

'Andrew's found a stray cat with four kittens,' I remembered. 'He's been buying cat food with his pocket money to save her having to go hunting for herself. But I don't know where it is.'

We tramped along the road and turned off into a narrow lane that led to the woods. 'Try to think,' Gwillym murmured. 'The cat will have found a shelter to have the kittens. It could be an old shed somewhere.'

'I don't think he said where the cat was,' I muttered. 'He just went off twice a day to feed her. I only found out because he took the tin opener, and the electric one broke, so Mum was looking everywhere for the other one. He said he'd borrowed it to open the cat food tins, and left it there.'

'He didn't say where?'

'I don't think so.'

'Well, it's probably nothing to do with the cat,' Gwillym said.

But it *was* important. I *knew* it was. The incident with the tin opener had happened last week, before I'd gone back to London for the weekend. I hadn't been paying attention to what anyone said or did – and now the boys' lives might depend on it!

We were walking down a narrow lane between high hedges, with deep ditches either side. Now and again, we stopped and called the boys' names, but no answer came. We reached the edge of the woodland and continued calling, and listening. Soon we could see the farmhouse through the trees because all the lights were on, and, as we emerged from the woods, we could see torchlights bobbing about here and there in the fields. 'All the Jones's are out looking for them,' Gwillym said. 'Someone will be sure to find them soon.'

'Not if they've fallen over the cliff,' I whispered.

'Peter is looking along the beaches, and I expect other people will be, too,' he answered. 'The other way they might have gone home from the farm, thinking it was a short cut, is up the hill towards the road. If we don't find them there, we'll call in at your house and see if your mother remembers anything about the cat.'

We set off along the rough ground that led back to the road. Now and again the moon came out and we could see outlines of bushes and trees. It gave me a little trickle of hope, because it really was easy to get lost in that total darkness. The boys wouldn't normally stay out until dark, but, as Gwillym reminded me, these dark clouds had descended so suddenly it could have caught them unawares. Yet I couldn't get rid of the feeling that they could be lying hurt somewhere, cold and frightened.

We reached the mill pond, and Gwillym said, 'Keep well away from the edge. It's very deep.'

'Oh, Gwillym!' I gasped. 'Could they have fallen in

the pond?' I shivered.

'They can swim,' he replied. 'They'd be able to get out.'

The moon sailed out from behind a cloud, showing the craggy outline of the old mill, gaunt and forbidding, derelict for years.

'Surely they wouldn't go in there!' I whispered, as I realized that Gwillym was going to check it. I thought of old rusty machinery that could have fallen and crushed them. I'd never been inside, but there were gaping holes where windows used to be and where doors had rotted away, and the old wheel stood idle with the mill race rushing past.

He didn't answer. He was holding my arm, guiding me around the edge of the mill pond, shining his torch on the black water to show me the edge. Suddenly, I stopped, and stared upwards. It might be a trick of the moonlight, my eyes having become accustomed to the darkness, but I thought I saw a flash of light high up on the stone wall.

'What is it?' Gwillym asked sharply. 'What did you see?'

'Look,' I murmured. 'Right up at the top. *Is* it a light?'

The mill was still some way off, across the wide pond. We both stared upwards, and then it came again – a tiny thread of light, so faint it could have been imagination. It seemed to flash three times, and was gone.

'It's a *signal*!' Gwillym gasped. 'S.O.S.' He cupped his hands to his mouth and yelled, '*William*!'

A faint cry answered, followed by another, and my heart gave a violent jerk as Gwillym began to run the last stretch, and I followed him, praying the moon wouldn't disappear again, because now I could see the edge of the treacherous mill pond as I pounded after Gwillym.

We were beside the old wall, breathless, craning to look up at the black hole where the thread of light still kept flashing on and off three times, then pausing, and flashing again.

'William! Andrew!' I shrieked, and then, I could hear William's voice. 'We're up here. In the granary. The stairs gave way and we can't get down.'

'Are you all right?'

'No, because we can't get down.'

The moon rode out again, and I could see them, two blurred white figures against the black rectangle, and so high up!

'We'll get you down,' Gwillym called. Already he was diving in through the black space where a door had been and I followed him. 'Shine your torch over here, Lorna,' Gwillym said. 'If the moon stays out we'll be able to see where . . . '

As if in answer to a prayer, the moon shone brighter and threw a shaft of light across the floor. Then I could see where the wooden staircase against the side of the wall had collapsed. The top half hung at an angle away from the wall.

Above me was a square black hole in the ceiling. Gwillym called up, 'Can you see the trap door hole? Don't move unless you can see it properly.'

'Yes,' William answered. 'The moon's come out now.'

There were footsteps overhead, and then their two faces appeared above us, peering down through the hole.

'Lorna! I *knew* you'd find us,' Andrew cried. 'I did my signal, but William's pencil torch isn't much use, and the batteries were going. I did 'S.O.S.' *millions* of times.'

'Yes — that's what we saw,' I answered, and there were tears streaming down my cheeks. They were both safe! I couldn't look at the broken stairs. They could have fallen from the top of them on to this stone floor!

'The cat's up here,' Andrew said. 'The stairs broke when William came up. He had to jump the last bit, and he *just* landed!'

Terror stabbed me like a knife. If he hadn't 'just landed' . . .

Gwillym was testing the wooden staircase. 'I'll have to go to the farm and borrow a ladder,' he said. 'There's nothing here that I can make the staircase safe with — no rope, nothing.'

'The wooden stairs are O.K.,' William said. 'I tested each one as I went up, but I forgot the iron bolts that hold the rail to the wall. They're rusty, and one of them broke when I was near the top.'

'You'll have to hang on for a bit longer,' Gwillym said. 'Lorna will stay with you while I go and borrow a ladder. I'll be as quick as I can.'

He took his torch, and I heard his footsteps pounding the hard ground outside. Now it was quiet and still in the old building. The moonlight shone on a thick wooden shaft which rose from floor to ceiling, and two pairs of huge mill stones. Andrew was giving a commentary on the mill, as if this was a perfectly normal situation.

'They used to haul the sacks up through this trap door, Lorna,' he said. 'There's a pulley up here, with a chain, and they hooked the sacks on, and . . . '

I didn't care, but I pretended to listen with interest.

'Is Dad mad at us?' William asked anxiously.

'No! But he's very worried,' I answered. 'He's out looking for you all over the village. Gwillym and I have been yelling our heads off in the woods. Lots of people are out looking for you – even the coastguard.'

'Wow!' Andrew gasped. 'The *coastguard*!'

It seemed like ages, but it could only have been about fifteen minutes, before we heard footsteps and masculine voices talking in Welsh. The relief was ecstatic!

Mr Jones was a short, stockily built man, with wide powerful shoulders. 'And what have you two terrible boys got up to now?' he demanded, looking up at the boys' grinning faces. 'Half the village out searching for you! Trying to get yourselves interviewed on television, are you?'

As he and Gwillym fixed up the ladder, he told me that Mrs Jones had telephoned Mum immediately, to tell her the boys were safe, and that Dad was now on his way.

I watched Gwillym at the top of the ladder, making sure that Andrew got a safe foothold. Soon Andrew's sturdy little body was descending confidently, followed by William, then Andrew was in my arms, saying, 'Don't cry, Lorna! Can I go back to get the cat and kittens? She won't be able to get down either, now, because the stairs are gone – and how will I ever get up there to feed her?'

'Where is she?' Gwillym asked. 'I'll go up and get her.'

He descended the ladder again, a protesting cat in one arm, and four kittens in the pockets of his jacket.

Andrew took the cat, explaining to her that she would have to come home with us, now.

'No,' Gwillym said. 'She'll have to be confined for a bit, or she'll start trekking back here, carrying the kittens, one by one. I'll take them home with me and put them in a cage until she's settled.'

When we got to Jones's farm, Dad had arrived with the car.

'We're sorry, Dad,' William said, 'causing all this trouble.'

Dad smiled at him, and ruffled Andrew's hair. 'One of these mornings,' he said, 'I shall look in the mirror and find that my hair's turned white overnight. Come on, let's get you home.'

'I'll go with Gwillym, Dad,' I said. 'to help with the cat.'

'Cat?' Dad asked. 'What cat?'

'Tell you on the way home, Dad,' William grinned.

Mrs Jones lent us a basket for the kittens, and I held the cat on my lap, getting scratched for my trouble as the car started. She was a pretty cat, fluffy-haired, black and white, with beautiful green eyes.'

At the vet's house, Gwillym opened up the surgery and found a cage, just as his father came in from a late call. We made the large cage comfortable with a piece of soft blanket, and added a supply of milk and food.

'Tell your brother he can come and visit the cat, any time,' Mr Evans said.

Gwillym walked with me to the gate and I thanked him for all he'd done, adding, 'and thank you for taking me out today. It was lovely.'

'You're not getting rid of me yet,' he smiled. 'I'll walk home with you.'

As we reached our gate, he said, It's been quite an eventful couple of days, hasn't it?'

'It certainly has!' I smiled up at him. 'First the field glasses in the tunnel, and now this – those boys have been a great nuisance to you.'

He laughed and then drew me close. 'They keep bringing us together,' he murmured. 'That's fine with me.'

I was still high on the relief of finding the boys, and still emotional, and Gwillym's face was close to mine. When he bent to kiss me, I put my arms around his neck, and this time the kiss lasted even longer . . .

He opened our gate for me. 'See you around,' he smiled.

Chapter 8

Next morning, at breakfast, you'd never have believed that the boys had been up long after midnight, or that they'd had a frightening experience. They were wide awake and full of chatter, while Mum and Dad and I were still trying to come to terms with the day.

Dad was checking his appointments in his Filofax, and he passed a note to me under the table, which said, 'Can you keep next Thurday afternoon free for our shopping trip?' I smiled and nodded.

Andrew was saying, 'When Lorna rescued Jack, Peter and Jack sent her lots of yellow roses.'

Mum nodded absently. 'Yes. They were beautiful.'

'Well,' Andrew went on, 'what should William and me give Gwillym for rescuing us?'

'William and I,' Dad corrected automatically, still flicking through his Filofax.

'I'll go and buy Gwillym some yellow roses, with ribbons,' William said, and roared with laughter.

Andrew frowned. 'But he won't want them. Guys don't want flowers. Mum, what shall we get for Gwillym?'

Mum said, 'Well, you see, he'd be embarrassed, because there's no way of repaying people for things like that.'

'We could clean his car,' William suggested, 'inside and out. Dad, can we borrow the car vacuum cleaner and polish and stuff?'

'Good idea,' Dad muttered, getting up. 'I'm calling in now, on my way to work, to thank Gwillym, and to offer to pay for the cat's board and lodging.'

'I'll come with you,' Andrew said. 'I'm calling in, too, to visit the cat and kittens.'

'You are not coming,' Dad said firmly. 'You can't just rush in there any old time!'

'But – *you're* rushing in, Dad!'

'No. I'm *calling*, before surgery starts. You've lumbered them with an extra animal to look after, so you go after morning surgery, and politely ask if you may visit the cat, and find out what times will be convenient.

'Yes, Dad,' Andrew muttered.

There was an insistent ring at the doorbell. I answered it to find a young red-haired guy who said he was a reporter from the weekly newspaper, and he wanted to interview the boys who'd been rescued from the old mill.

'Er – I'm not sure,' I answered. 'Wait here. I'll have to ask Dad.'

When I told him, Dad said, '*What*? They must be short of hard news! No – it's bad enough, having roused half the village, without having the story in the newspaper.'

Mum looked up at him and said, 'Steve – there's just one thing. If if could warn other boys to be careful of old buildings . . . If it alerts parents to what can happen . . . '

Dad hesitated. 'I hadn't thought of that. Perhaps . . . Yes, all right then.'

I went to tell the reporter that he could come in. 'Great!' he grinned. 'I'll get the photographer. He's waiting in the car.'

'Mum,' I asked, 'is it all right if I go and see Peter, to thank him for searching for the boys last night?'

She smiled. 'You mean you don't want to see your photograph in the Gwenally Gazette on Saturday?'

I grinned. 'No way!'

'Well, tell Peter how deeply grateful we all are,' she said.

Peter's studio looked much larger. The life-size sculpture 'Family Group' had gone to the foundry to be cast in bronze.

Peter was working at a machine in the corner, feeding in lumps of clay from a bin, which came out at the other end of the machine in a long smooth cylinder. 'I've always wondered what that machine did,' I said.

'It's called a pugmill,' he explained. 'Clay that's been used can be used again, but first it has to be compressed so that all the air is squeezed out of it, and it's made soft again, without any lumps. Have some coffee?'

'No thanks, I've just had breakfast.' I gave him Mum's message. 'I'm sorry the boys caused so much trouble for so many people last night,' I said.

'Nonsense! This is what living in a village is all about. People *wanted* to help. Did you have a good day with Gwillym, before you got home and found the boys were missing?'

'Oh yes,' I smiled. 'We never stopped talking!'

'Did you tell him about Mike?'

'*No!*' I gasped. 'I don't know him well enough to discuss — well, personal things, like that. Besides, he might have thought I wanted another boyfriend, and you know how I feel about that!'

'Yes,' he answered seriously.

'I suppose you feel the same,' I said quietly.

He hesitated. 'At the moment, yes. But that will pass.' He dumped more clay into the pugmill and it buzzed away as we talked.

'Are you sure it will pass?' I asked.

'It has to, doesn't it? People couldn't go on living if everything that happened went on hurting for ever. The burden would become intolerable. Everything that happens, good or bad, changes us a bit. The bad things make us tougher, if we let them.'

He cut off the roll of clean smooth clay which had emerged from the pugmill, put it into a plastic bag, and switched off the machine.

'Just imagine,' he said, 'how you'd feel, if Mike drove down here today, and begged you to forgive him for going out with Zara, and said he wanted to have a really serious relationship with you.'

I thought about it. 'I couldn't trust him,' I said. 'Besides, I don't want to go through all that again; living every moment for someone else, being only half alive when they're not there.'

'Being only half alive,' Peter murmured. 'Yes. You put things very well, Lorna. But I promise you, you'll get over the shock, and then you'll feel differently about boys. There'll be someone else, and you'll love him more than you ever loved Mike.'

'No!' I said sharply. 'I could never love anyone else the way I loved Mike!'

I was leaning against the wall, beside the bin which held the used clay, ready for the pugmill, and I glanced down at it and, among the unrecognizable lumps, I saw a shape, and realized it was the portrait of Megan! My eyes flew to the shelf where it had been, and now there was an empty space.

'*Peter*!' I whispered, horrified, 'you could have finished it from memory! How *can* you put it through the pugmill?'

'I couldn't look at it any more,' he said simply.

Then I remembered that I'd put Mike's photo away, along with the gifts which I'd once treasured so much. 'I'm sorry, Peter,' I murmured. 'It was just so beautiful.'

'Part of the past,' he said, 'to be re-used, just as our experiences should be re-used, if we learn from them. You're trying to cut yourself off, Lorna, instead of making use of experience.'

I went to perch on the arm of the sofa. I couldn't watch pieces of that sculpture being tossed into the pugmill, even though I wanted to hate Megan for what she'd done to Peter.

'Peter,' I said, 'I don't ever want to be like I was, when I was separated from Mike, before we finally parted. I didn't care about anyone else, only Mike. I made things difficult for Mum and Dad, and I couldn't be bothered with the boys. I was *horrible*!'

He switched on the pugmill again, and went on talking quietly. 'When Megan told me she was going to marry Andy Miller,' he said, 'I felt as if my life was over. When I was alone here, I wanted to break everything in sight.

'Instead, I took Jack for a walk along the cliffs, at

three o'clock in the morning. As you get older, you see, you learn to cope. And you helped me a lot.'

'*What?*' I nearly overbalanced from the arm of the sofa. 'You *can't* mean that!'

'But I do. You listened, and understood. I've told no one else, yet. I only wish you'd let me help *you*, by believing what I tell you. If you go on trying to blank out your feelings, you'll waste a lot of your youth, miss a lot of fun, and stay very vulnerable.'

On the way home, I saw William and Andrew in the drive of the vet's house, with two plastic pails, busily washing Gwillym's car. Andrew dropped his cloth and came rushing to me. 'You missed *everything*!' he shouted, while he was still yards away. 'We had our photos taken, and William and me are going to be in the newspaper on Saturday.'

'So,' I grinned, 'on Saturday morning, there'll be a crowd outside our house wanting your autograph!'

'Don't be silly!' he giggled. 'But guess what? Gwillym is taking us to Pentreath Bay this afternoon, to see the sailing ships that are in the film, and he says you can come, too, if you like. I told him you would want to come, because you were in the school drama group, and crackers about actors like Michael J. Fox and Tom Cruise.'

'Oh, did you really?' I muttered, wishing Andrew would learn to keep his mouth shut occasionally.

Mum was making coffee when I went indoors, and I suddenly remembered the green jug I'd bought for her yesterday. So much had happened since that I'd completely forgotten it.

She was really pleased with it. 'I'll use it for flowers,' she said. 'Isn't it strange how you and I have similar taste?'

'We both have this feeling for the finer things in life,' I said.

'That must be it,' she nodded, and we both giggled.

There was a ring at the doorbell. 'Oh, not that reporter again!' Mum groaned.

It was Gwillym at the door. Mum poured coffee for him and began saying how grateful we all were. He stopped her, insisting it was pure luck, then asked if both of us would like to go to Pentreath Bay to see the filming.

'It's very kind of you to include me, Gwillym,' Mum said, 'I'd love to come, but there's a meeting this afternoon about the church fête on Saturday.'

'I'd like to come,' I said. 'Are you sure you can stand a whole afternoon of my brothers' company – after the trouble they've caused you?'

He laughed. 'They're doing an amazing job on my car.'

When the boys came in to lunch, William said, 'Gwillym's just as clever with cars as Mike. He's fitted new doors, new rear bumper, and had it re-sprayed at Carter's garage. It's eight years old, and worth the re-spray. Automatic gearbox, fuel injection, electronic ignition . . .'

I switched off. This was all too familiar. And now I knew why I hadn't noticed how much Mike went on about cars. I'd switched off and kept nodding. I was doing it now. Then Andrew said something which made me switch on again and glare at him across the table.

'What did you say?' I demanded.

'I told Gwillym all about Mike,' he repeated cheerfully.

I froze. '*What* did you tell him?'

'That he was mad about cars, that's all.'

I relaxed and went on with my lunch, then Andrew said, 'William, why did you kick me and send me for clean water when the water didn't need changing?'

'I — I didn't kick hard,' William muttered, his face turning pink.

I laid down my fork. 'What was he saying?' I asked warily.

'Nothing really,' William mumbled.

'Andrew,' I asked menacingly, 'what were you saying when William kicked you?'

'Only that Mum told us not to bother you when we first came here, because you were very sad at leaving Mike.'

I groaned. 'Thanks a lot, Andrew. Any more?'

He screwed up his eyes, as if trying to remember. 'When William kicked me, I think I was saying that you didn't want Mike any more, because you'd put his photo away and stopped playing 'Flip Side of Loving' all the time, so if Gwillym wanted to be your boyfriend, I thought it would be O.K. to ask you.'

William said, 'Lorn, I don't think Gwillym was listening. He was fixing the brake light, and you know how Andrew goes on . . . '

Mum was trying to explain to Andrew that he

121

mustn't talk about personal and family matters outside the family.

I muttered, 'I'd feel a lot safer if he wore a gag all the time and only took if off to eat.'

When Gwillym arrived, after lunch, the boys were delighted to see Jack sitting beside him, in the car.

'You don't mind if we take him?' Gwillym asked me. 'Peter has to go to Cardiff this afternoon to see an architect about a commission. He didn't want to leave Jack shut up alone in the house.'

I wore my green and white striped dress with my green leather sandals. Gwillym looked terrific in a deep blue shirt and black jeans.

Andrew said, 'You do look nice, Lorna. That dress reminds me of peppermint rock.'

I thought wistfully of the gag, and turned to Gwillym whose eyes were bright with laughter. 'If I look like a stick of peppermint rock,' I said grimly, 'you'll have to wait while I go and change.'

'Don't you dare!' Gwillym answered. 'You look cool and lovely.' Then, as we got into the car, he added, with a wicked grin, 'Besides, I love peppermint rock.'

We set off along the same route that Gwillym and I had taken the day before. The weather was still glorious, the boys' enthusiasm infectious, and the big black dog sat happily between them on the back seat. The hind leg in plaster seemed not to bother him at all.

After nearly an hour's drive, Gwillym parked the car in a leafy lane, and carried Jack down the steeply sloping path which wound through dense woodland to emerge on to a stretch of golden bracken, where he set the dog down and clipped on his leash.

Andrew was, for once, speechless, at the sight of two fully rigged sailing ships riding at anchor off the shore. Before us was a small horseshoe-shaped bay, with a wide strip of pale sand, where woodland swept down to the sea on either side. On the verge of the sand was a row of white fishermen's cottages backed by a grove of trees.

The cottages had been skilfully aged by several hundred years, and the sand was littered with casks, fishing nets, and upturned rowing boats. Wooden planks had been laid on the sand for the mobile cameras.

A barrier had been erected to keep sightseers at bay, but we were the only sightseers as we moved up to the barrier and William took Jack's leash.

The dog sat obediently, head alert, watching the actors grouped around a man wearing a white shirt, jeans, and horn-rimmed glasses, who looked incongruous among people wearing eighteenth century costume.

People with clip-boards hovered anxiously, then the scene was cleared except for two actors in dark jerseys, breeches, and high leather boots, who took a rowing boat a little way out to sea, then turned and rowed back while the cameras tracked them.

Gwillym whispered, 'The girl sitting in the cottage doorway – that's Megan Price.'

She was *lovely*! She wore a long scarlet skirt and white blouse, and her black hair fell to her waist. She was sitting on the doorstep of the cottage, sewing some dark material. At a cue from the man in the white shirt, she dropped her sewing and ran to the water's edge.

The two men leapt out of the boat, one of them splashing through the water to embrace Megan, the other pulling the boat in. The camera followed Megan and the man she greeted, as they walked slowly back to the cottage, the man's arm around Megan's waist.

Suddenly, a third actor appeared, came up behind the man walking with Megan, grabbed him roughly by the shoulder and spun him round. Megan looked at the attacker, and screamed.

In that instant, Jack took off like a rocket, jerking the leash from William's hand, and tearing off at amazing speed on his three good legs. As we watched, frozen with horror, he leapt at the man who had attacked Megan's escort, knocking him over, then stood, with his paws on the man's chest, growling.

Megan recognized Jack, flung her arms around him and collapsed with laughter, while the dog returned her greeting with wild barks and tail waving, as the actor got to his feet.

Before we could move, Andrew had dived under the barrier and raced on to the set to grab the dog, while confusion raged, with people yelling, 'Cut!' 'Where did that dog come from?' 'Get that boy off the set!'

Gwillym and I dived under the barrier, followed by William, as the man in the white shirt grabbed Andrew by the shoulders and shook him, roaring, 'Get away from here, boy, and take your wretched dog with you. Don't let me catch you around here again!'

Gwillym dashed forward. 'Take your hands off

him!' he snapped, stepping between the man and Andrew. 'He doesn't even know why it happened.'

'Who cares *why* it happened?' the man shouted. 'It *happened*, didn't it?'

Megan and the other actors were still laughing. It seemed everyone was either amused or furious.

Megan looked up from where she was sitting on the sand, fondling Jack's ears. She was still breathless with laughter as she said, 'Hello, Gwillym! What's Jack doing here?'

Gwillym explained, while the man in the white shirt took off his glasses and wiped his brow and said, 'How can we work in these circumstances? Megan, if you think this is funny—'

'Oh, shut up, Michael,' Megan said. 'It's only one "take". The dog knows me, and when I screamed, he came to rescue me – which is more than a lot of you creeps would have done!' She glared at the technicians who were still muttering angrily.

The director continued to moan about wasted time and money, and Megan sighed, 'Michael, you'd have wanted at least three more "takes" of that scene. And we're overdue for a break.'

'O.K.,' the man muttered sullenly. 'We'll take a half hour break. Somebody bring some coffee – quickly!'

Gwillym introduced the boys and me to Megan, and we all began apologizing.

'It doesn't matter,' she insisted. 'This is our very last location scene, and it was time for a break.'

The actor who'd been knocked over by Jack was introduced to us as Philip Carson, but we'd already recognized him because we'd all seen him on television. Several of the other actors looked familiar, too, and the one who'd walked with Megan back towards the cottage was Tom Granger, who'd starred in lots of things on television.

Andrew was asking Tom Granger about the ships, and if he'd actually been aboard. The actor explained that the smaller ship was made of fibre glass and was used for deck scenes and background, but that the larger one was genuine.

'There's a proper crew here, permanently,' he explained, 'to handle the ships for the film. Shall I ask one of them to take you on board?'

'Oh, *please!*' Andrew breathed, his eyes shining.

Soon, a huge bronzed man called Jem, was rowing the boys out to the ship, while we sat on the sand talking to Megan, Philip Carson, and Tom Granger, and drinking coffee out of plastic cups.

'Are those the only two ships you've used in the film?' I asked.

'Isn't two enough?' Megan smiled.

I laughed. 'I saw a sailing ship pass Caeraddon Bay,' I explained. 'But it wasn't like either of those. Andrew saw it too. He said it was a brig.'

Tom Granger said, 'Neither of those is a brigantine. The big one is a schooner, and the fake one is a barque.'

I intercepted a glance between Megan and Gwillym, and Gwillym said. 'I told her the legend, Megan, but she doesn't believe in it any more than I do. We think the ship she saw must be being used as a training vessel further along the coast.'

Megan nodded. 'I believe these ships are sometimes

used for adventure holidays, too, for people mad enough to want to learn to sail them.'

'The ship I saw,' I said, 'was black, and it was flying a red flag. Before I had chance to look at it properly it was gone – out of sight.'

Megan looked up at me suddenly. Our eyes met, and I knew that she believed in the legend.

'I thought I saw the Dark Lady once,' she said. 'I was twelve years old. Three days later, I fell overboard from a yacht. Daddy just got to me in time. They say that good old Henry Standing does his best for you. If you get into trouble despite his warning, he'll try to help you. But I expect he'd rather you saved him the trouble.' She spoke lightly, with amusement in her voice, then she glanced out sea, and asked, 'When did Andrew see the brig?'

'Eleven days ago,' I answered.

'So he's safe now,' she said. 'And you?'

'I saw it last Wednesday.'

'So you must tread carefully for three more days,' she smiled. 'No motor racing, no parachute jumping.'

'I won't even go big-game hunting,' I promised.

Tom Granger said, 'When the boys come back, it would be a good idea if you took the dog away, in case he does it again, or barks furiously, so it comes through on the soundtrack.'

Gwillym nodded. 'Don't worry,' he said, 'we'll get him out of range of Megan's scream.'

We talked for a while longer, then Megan was called for by the make-up people, and at that moment we saw the rowing boat returning.

Gwillym drove inland to Pentreath village, where

the annual agricultural show was being held in the grounds of a ruined castle. There was enough of the castle left to interest the boys, then we went on to the show and wandered around looking at the exhibitions of craftwork until William noticed that we were in time for the finals of the dog trials, which he was sure Jack would like to see.

Jack watched with deep interest while other dogs leapt through hoops and retrieved objects, and demonstrated obedience to commands.

'You could do all that,' William told him confidently. 'No problem.'

We stayed for another hour, then Gwillym had to take us home, because he'd promised to help his father with the evening surgery.

The boys needed no prompting to thank him wholeheartedly for 'A super time!', telling him it had been, 'Absolutely *Ace*! *Brill*!'

Andrew hung on our gate, watching Gwillym's car disappear down the road, murmuring, 'Magic! That schooner was *magic*!'

Chapter 9

On Thursday afternoon, Dad and I didn't have to go further than Gwenally to find exactly what I knew Mum would like for her present. The shop had a huge selection of antique jewellery, and I chose a pretty Victorian silver ring set with an oval ruby surrounded by tiny diamonds.

I'd told Mum I was going into Gwenally to buy some tights, so I went and bought them, then Dad drove me back to Caeraddon. He was going to wait in the village until I'd had ample time to get home, them come in himself, saying he'd got away from work early for a change.

I was half way down the hill when Gwillym drew up in his car beside me, and took me home, so I let him into the secret and asked him in for tea.

We were laughing about something as we went through the hall to the kitchen. I can't remember what it was, because, there, sitting at the kitchen table with Mum, was Mike!

Panic flared through me. What if he'd come, as Peter had suggested he might, to tell me he'd changed his mind about us? I stared at him, too shocked to speak.

Mum rescued me, introducing him to Gwillym as 'Mike Kingston, a friend of Lorna's, touring Wales on a camping holiday. As he was so near, he decided to drop in. Do sit down, Gwillym.'

'No, thank you, Mrs Collins,' Gwillym replied. 'I have to get home to help Dad – with his assistant, Glenys, still away on holiday, you know.'

As Gwillym left, Mum remembered some urgent phone calls she had to make, and I tried to control my shaking hand as I poured tea for Mike.

'Where are you camping?' I asked, as he helped himself to a piece of cake. 'And where's your car?'

'I left the car in that garage in the village,' he said. 'They're fixing the door handle. They said it was only a five minute walk to your house, so it fitted in nicely.'

Relief spread through me. So he didn't intend to stay long!

'Are you – alone?' I asked.

'No. Nick, the guy whose room you saw, is with me. We brought Nick's tent and my car. Nick's visiting an aunt in Cardiff today, so I thought I'd look you up. I mean – we're still friends, aren't we?'

I gazed at him, meeting the full impact of the grey eyes that looked at me teasingly. He'd acquired a deep golden tan, and his hair was streaked blond by the sun. He looked like an advert for health foods, or exercise equipment – too good to be real, somehow, in a red shirt and faded denims.

'I certainly understand,' he said, 'why you were desperate to get away from here!'

I thought, I was desperate to be with you, but I said, 'You do?'

He nodded. 'We've been in the area for about a week. There's nothing happening here! It's O.K. in this good weather, lazing around, swimming, but what do they do in the evenings?'

I didn't answer. I didn't need to. He went on talking.

'Your mother's still a first class cook,' he said, finishing the cake and taking a jam tart. 'She looks younger – this place suits her. Of course, it's fine for retirement, isn't it? And older people don't need entertainment. They've got television.'

I heard Dad come in, and Mum's surprised greeting, then lowered voices as they went into the living room and shut the door.

Mike went on eating and talking. 'I drove through a place near here called Gwen something. It's really creepy! Dead! I thought, "Well, if this is where it all happens!" And the village! O.K. on picture postcards, but to have to *live* here, for *real*! No wonder you got so uptight about it.'

I was surprised by the anger that stirred inside me. Coldly, I said, 'You've got to go further afield to find a sports centre, or a theatre, perhaps. But there are other ways of spending your free time here.'

'Such as?' he bit into another jam tart, looking at me with amusement. 'Don't tell me you've gone all rustic! Is that why you hated Nick's room? Turned into a country girl, have you?' He laughed incredulously, and I felt like hitting him.

'It's a nice house though,' he acknowledged. 'Lorna – I'm picking Nick up in Swansea this evening. I expect you know some girls here. Why don't you ring someone, and we'll make up a foursome for tonight? You can show us the night-spots!' he laughed, mockingly.

'Sorry,' I snapped. 'I don't know anyone who'd want to come.'

He leaned back in his chair. 'You're still mad at me! But, Lorna, you can't blame me for not wanting a heavy relationship – especially the way things are. With you down here and me in London, there'd have been no future in it, would there?'

'None at all,' I agreed bitterly.

'Right! So ring a girlfriend, and come out with Nick and me for old time's sake. It would be a real treat for a local girl, and there's bound to be a decent disco in a town the size of Swansea.'

'Even if I wanted to do a local girl a big favour,' I said icily, 'I don't know any of them yet.'

'O.K.,' he nodded. 'I'll tell Nick to amuse himself for the evening. You and I can go out – just the two of us, have a meal, catch up on the news . . . '

I was slowly shaking my head. 'I'm busy tonight,' I said.

He stood up and looked at his watch. 'I get the message,' he snapped. 'The car will be ready now. I'm sorry you feel this way, Lorna. When you're older, you'll be able to see things in perspective, take the longer view.'

'Meaning,' I murmured, 'that I'm immature?'

'Well,' he grinned, 'I really do think, Lorna, that it is about time you grew up.'

Without realizing it, I'd stood up, too. We were about a foot apart, and when my hand came up and slapped his face, I was as surprised as he was.

It was a hard slap, and his head jerked, then he put

his fingers to his cheek, amazed. 'That proves it!' he growled angrily. 'You're just a spoiled kid!'

'And you,' I flared at him, 'are conceited, arrogant, insensitive, and *insulting*! So go away and find some other way of filling up the evening.'

'Right!' he snapped.

He turned and strode through the hall, and the front door slammed. I dashed up to my room and flung myself on the bed. Why was I crying? Why was I pounding the pillow with my fists, as if it was Mike I was trying to knock some feeling into? He wasn't worth it. If I knew nothing else, I knew that, now!

By the time Mum called up that dinner was ready, I'd calmed down and changed into jeans and an old tee shirt. *Why* had I let Mike get to me? Maybe I really did need to grow up. But – how? How do you manage not to feel hurt and angry when someone criticizes things he knows nothing about – things you're fond of? When he'd sneered at the village, I'd wanted to scream at him that it was people who mattered – people who'd come out to help when the boys were missing, and who'd been kind and friendly to us.

When he'd said Gwenally was dead, I could have told him that I'd had one magic evening there that I'd always remember, when a boy who was kind and gentle, and popular, had stood up on stage and sung in a voice that went straight to the heart. And Mike wouldn't have understood one word of what I was saying.

Later in the evening, I went upstairs to get my book on myths and legends of Wales, and found Andrew in my room, in his pyjamas.

'What are you doing here?' I demanded angrily.

'Nothing,' he muttered. 'Just — looking.'

'Looking at *what*?'

'Nothing, because it isn't there.'

This was getting ridiculous. '*What* isn't there?'

'Mike's photo. I was only looking to see if you'd put it back.'

I glared down at him. 'And what has that got to do with you?' I snapped.

'A lot,' he muttered. 'Mum said he'd been here today.'

'So?'

'If *he's* come back, you'll start being like you were when we weren't supposed to bother you, and I *hate* that! Unless he's coming to live here, too. Then you won't be like that; only Mum said he was just visiting, so—'

'He's gone now,' I said. 'Go back to bed and don't come in here again without asking.'

He looked up at me accusingly. 'You see?' he said. 'You don't usually talk to me like that. It's because *he's* come back! I just wish he'd go right away — to, to *India*, and live there for ever!'

Despite my irritation, I almost smiled. 'Why India?'

'It's the longest way off I can think of,' he replied. 'And I expect they've got cars, so he'd be all right!'

He stormed out of the room and slammed the door, leaving me feeling guilty that I'd shouted at him.

I didn't see Gwillym all day on Friday, but I had plenty to do. Mum's car had been delivered at last, a red Mini, and I went out with her, collecting things for her stall at the church fête.

Saturday morning was marked by the arrival of the Gwenally Gazette, with pictures of the boys on the front page. "Dramatic rescue story inside", the caption read.

On the centre pages, the cat and kittens looked appealing, and the old mill looked grim and forbidding. A headline yelled, "BOY'S KNOWLEDGE OF MORSE CODE SAVES LIVES".

"From afar", we read, "the boys' sister, Lorna (16), and her boyfriend, Gwillym Evans (18), frantically searching the area, saw a tiny thread of light flashing rhythmically – S.O.S.! With only a pencil torch and fading batteries, Andrew (10), managed to send out the vital signal."

I had to admire the way in which the reporter had managed to make the article dramatic, sensational, and harrowing – "The boys were themselves on a rescue mission, taking food bought out of their pocket money to a stray cat marooned there with her four kittens . . . "

'Doesn't that reporter tell whopping lies?' William murmured.

'Who told him that Gwillym was my boyfriend?' I demanded. 'What's he going to think when he reads this?'

I helped Mum with her bric-a-brac stall at the church fête in the afternoon. We were frantically busy for the first hour, then no one wanted to buy what was left – some framed pictures and vases and lampshades.

The boys roamed the side-shows, and I went to look at the other stalls, and found Nerys Griffiths and Sian Hughes, the two girls I'd met at the folk club, running the flower stall.

They told me about a barbecue, arranged by the parent-teacher's association for Sunday afternoon in the headmistress's garden. 'It's for anyone connected with the school,' Nerys said. 'It starts at five. *Do* come, Lorna. You can bring a friend. Bring Gwillym.'

'There's Gwillym!' Sean said, 'at your Mum's stall.'

I hoped it didn't show that my heart had done a funny little skip and begun beating faster. I tried not to hurry as I walked back to the stall.

Gwillym was buying all the pictures, because he wanted the frames. It was six o'clock now, and the stalls were being dismantled. The boys wanted to stay and help, and Mum had to stay to pay in the money we'd taken. 'But you go with Gwillym, Lorna, if you like,' she said.

'O.K. – I'll go and get supper started,' I agreed. Dad was working on the garden at home, and he'd be glad not to have to wait too long for a meal.

As we walked across the field to Gwillym's car, I said, anxiously. 'I'm sorry about that newspaper article, Gwillym. That reporter had no right to—'

'I haven't seen it yet,' he answered. 'I've been to visit my grandmother in Carmarthen, and stopped by the fête on my way home. What are you sorry about?'

'It's wildly exaggerated,' I muttered. 'It – it says you're my boyfriend!'

He opened the car door for me, and as I got in, he

said, 'And what does Mike think about that?'

'*Mike?*' I looked at him, surprised.

He got into the car and started the engine. 'I expect he's pretty mad about that,' he said.

'Mike and I parted, ages ago!' I gasped. 'The other day, he was just passing — on holiday — and he called in.'

'Oh! I thought he was staying with you, on a visit,' Gwillym said.

'No way!' I muttered darkly.

Gwillym smiled, and stopped the car for the traffic lights as we came out of Gwenally. He said, 'I didn't come around yesterday, because I thought — and anyway, I thought maybe you'd seen enough of me for a while.'

'I wish you *had* come,' I said. 'We don't always have to go out. We could have played cassettes, or just talked.'

'You really mean that?' He was looking me intently. The lights had changed, and people behind us were sounding their horns.

'The lights, Gwillym,' I reminded him, and he drove on, and I said, 'Of *course* I mean it.'

I watched his profile and saw the smile that made his dark eyes light up. I wanted to move closer to him, to touch him. It wasn't going to be easy, being cool and distant. I'm just not made that way.

Could Peter be right? But — what if it all went wrong, just because I let Gwillym see how much I liked him? It made Mike back off, didn't it? I must never be "possessive" again. But Gwillym wasn't Mike. Mike had made me afraid to show my feelings.

All the same, I asked Gwillym if he'd like to go to the barbecue tomorrow, and he agreed straight away.

On Sunday, when Gwillym came for me at half past four, Mum suggested that we ought not to stay out too late, as it was my first day at school tomorrow.

'It'll finish quite early,' Gwillym said. 'We'll be home before dark.'

The headmistress, Miss Grayson, had a huge garden, and the smell of frying sausages met us as we went in through the gate. Nerys and Sean came over and introduced their boyfriends, then Nerys pointed out some of the teachers who'd be taking our form. It seemed strange, mixing socially with teachers, like this. In London we'd never seen our teachers outside school.

Miss Grayson recognized me, and took me to meet Miss Stephens, who'd be my form mistress. I liked her straight away. 'You may find we do things differently from what you're used to,' she said, 'so, if you have any problems, come and find me, and we'll sort things out between us.'

Time whizzed by as we sat on the grass, eating sausages and baked potatoes with Nerys and Sean and their boyfriends, David and Emlyn, both of whom were going to university soon. We talked about our families, and about films that were showing locally, which I'd seen ages ago, in London, with Mike, though I was careful not to say so. When it was time to leave, Nerys and Sean said, 'See you in the morning,' to me, and Sean called after me, 'Don't be late!'

As we drove home, Gwillym sighed. 'It's a pity you start tomorrow, and I don't start till Thursday. Can I come over for a bit tomorrow evening, just to see how you get on?'

'Oh yes!' I agreed. 'Surely there won't be too much homework on the first day!'

He stopped the car at our front gate and we got out, and wandered across to the cliff edge. The sun was beginning to set, spreading a path of gold across the sea and tinting the sky with gold and rose. On the horizon, a small fishing fleet looked like tiny black toy boats against the flame colours of the sky.

Gwillym said, 'I'll teach you an old local custom – to wish the fishermen good luck.' He held up the first finger of his right hand, and placed the first finger of his left hand against it, to make the form of a cross, looked out at the fishing boats and said, 'We wish you good luck, and a safe return.'

I did the same, as I watched the little boats making for the open sea and dangerous deep waters.

Gwillym murmured. 'I promised your mother we'd be home before dark.'

He took my hand and we walked slowly back to our gate, where he took me in his arms and held me close. I laid my head on his shoulder, and wanted to stay there for ever, full of a strange new sense of joy. When he kissed me, I wasn't afraid any more. Gwillym would never hurt me, and I could never bear to hurt him. I just couldn't stay cool and distant with him.

Before we parted, he looked down at me, and whispered, 'Lorna – I love you.'

And I looked up into those wonderful dark eyes, so full of expression, and said what I'd sworn I would never say again. 'I love you, too, Gwillym.'

I stayed by the gate, watching his car until it swung into his own drive, then I turned and looked up at the house, remembering how I'd hated it when we first came here.

I'd never forget this summer, full of so many experiences — bitterness, heartbreak, and now, at last, happiness, and love! And tomorrow would be a new beginning, with new friends.

My life was starting all over again! I walked up the path, still wrapped in a deep sense of peace and joy. I looked up at the old house, strong and secure, and knew that I could think of it now as home — and it was good to be home. Home before dark.

Barbara Jacobs
Two Times Two £1.50

Just what kind of dreams they were, Joanne was determined to find out. Kim had changed completely and would not talk about the mysterious new boyfriend whose presence now threatens their friendship. However, Paolo is not all that they imagine. Smooth, charming and *very* good looking, he begins to make Joanne feel that *she* is the only one who really understands his problems . . .

Joanne's decision to protect her friend sets off a chain of events that can only destroy everything that matters to her – including her own romance with art student Tony . . .

Mary Hooper
Love, Emma XXX £1.25

Emma begins her nursing training with high hopes. Determined to achieve something for herself, she still finds the three-year separation from her established world of family and friends a little frightening. In letters to her parents, best friend and boyfriend – and in entries in her secret diary – Emma describes her new world in warm and witty detail . . . hard-working, occasionally exciting and always exhausting – but there are rewards; *and* a student doctor named Luke . . .

Mary Hooper
Happy Ever After £1.25

Marcy is a romantic and when her sister, Sooty, announces her engagement the wedding becomes the most important thing in her life. Her own fantasies centre on Mick, the good-looking boy who works next door to her, and, when they meet and like each other, she longs for it to be 'forever and a day'. But real life has many unexpected twists of plot and when the dreamed-of moment comes, Marcy makes a surprising decision . . .

Ann Ruffell
Friends for Keeps £1.25

Clive was twenty, sophisticated, fantastic-looking, and different from anyone Frankie had ever known. But when he asked her out, Frankie knew she could never take him home to meet her mother. Not subject him to one of those embarrassing family discussions that could range from politics to the pill. At first he treated her reluctance to take him home with amusement, but when he started to suspect that she was two-timing him, she had to explain a lot more than she'd bargained for – like her relationship with Alan.

David S. Williams
Forgive and Forget £1.25

Claire's life was in turmoil when her family moved to Wales. It meant leaving Simon, the guy who meant so much to her, and she was determined *never* to like her new home. But the rugged beauty of the countryside and the compelling friendliness of the people soothed away her resentment. And then she met Gareth, a dark-eyed Welsh boy who captivated her with his infectious grin . . .

Lorna Read
Images 95p

Belinda's friends are mad with jealousy when she lands a holiday job working for a company that manages pop groups. But the fact that she isn't a raving pop fan got her the job in the first place, and she remains calm and level-headed – until the day singer Flip Sauvage walks up to the Reception desk . . .